MY ONLY ONE

BOOK 1

FORTUNATO FAMILY SERIES

CHARLOTTE O'SHAY

CHARLOTTE O'SHAY
ROMANCE

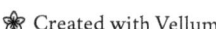

DEDICATION

To Patricia, my friend since first grade. You're an amazing combination of intelligence and compassion, one of the most beautiful and fun people I've ever known. You, a doctor, couldn't understand why I, a lawyer, would switch careers to become a romance author but you always read my books and called yourself a fan. Holly and Ivy (who will each get their own stories in this series) were inspired by the ear worm you gave me back in third grade when you sang Christmas in Killarney non-stop. I can't believe you're gone.

EPIGRAPH

"If you are more fortunate than others, it is better to build a longer table than a taller fence."
    ~Unknown

CHAPTER 1

ESME

Audentis Fortuna Iuvat
Fortune Favors the Brave

DON'T STOP RUNNING... *Don't stop running...*
My blood pounded with the chant, the words keeping time with my heartbeat, my ragged breaths and my footfalls on the pavement. Yes, footfalls. I was running on filthy New York City concrete on bare feet. But my dirty, cut up feet were the least of my troubles.

Don't stop till you get home.

First thing I'd do when I got home was give Papá a giant piece of my mind for everything he hadn't told me about tonight. For blindsiding me with his deception. I'd gone to that hotel tonight ready to do the unthinkable. I'd steeled myself to meet his *friend* because our backs were against the wall. Our money was gone. But my father deliberately left out vital information and now that I'd run, we could both get killed.

When I got home, I'd keep a rein on my temper and ignore the hurt. I had to. Giving in to anger, wallowing in the painful knowledge of my father's deceit, would only cloud my thinking the way my naivety had blinded me tonight. No matter how much I deserved to, I couldn't waste time with what-the-hell-were-you-thinkings when we had to get out —fast.

Packing our clothes would be simple because we didn't own a single thing of value anymore. We'd sold our only keepsake of Mama, her piano, after she passed. It was too painful for us to hear the silence every day. Besides we finally had no choice but to let it go. Every time we'd moved and we'd moved a lot during the last ten years, we spent money we didn't have transporting the piano to wherever our latest apartment was, which allowed Mama the comfort of playing till her last days. You might think we fetched a decent sum for the old Baldwin upright but even though plenty of people called to express interest when I posted an online neighborhood ad, no one had a way to get it down four flights of stairs. In the end we practically gave it away. So there was nothing we'd miss and no reminders of Mama in our current place, a studio whose sole virtue was its manageable rent— paid monthly in cash. My mind was made up. My father and I would head up to the Port Authority tonight and hop a bus headed as far from the city as we could get.

Because only a fool would run out on Reinaldo Rojas, then stick around to gauge his reaction. I wasn't a fool. Foolishly naive? I guess I used to be, but not anymore.

I winced, pain shooting up my shin as I stepped off the curb. Even though I was carrying, not wearing my stilettos, I never saw the ridge of cracked sidewalk on Eleventh Avenue till I slammed flat on top of it. I crashed hard onto the unforgiving cement, scraping both knees and one elbow. Gaining my feet, all adrenalin, I ignored my raw skin with its thick, oozing trickles of blood coated with a thick schmear of New

York City street grit. No way would I stop till I was home. *Keep going.*

These stupid shoes. Determined to look appropriately sophisticated tonight, I'd worn the stilettos I lucked onto on a high-end consignment website. Gorgeous works of art for the feet, they were all soft silk and buttery leather. They fit like they were made expressly for me and in truth I never would've had an excuse to buy them if not for tonight's event. But now I cursed the impulse to gift myself such an extravagance even though Papá went on and on about the importance of making a favorable impression. Which I took to mean— try not to look like we rented a fourth floor walkup on the lower east side. But really, Papá? I'd found out the person I went there to meet knew exactly how much money we had. Or, in our case, didn't have. The dumpster fire disaster of our life right now was the direct result of my epic naivety and my father's shaming inability to confide in me the whole truth about the precarious—no—dangerous situation we found ourselves in.

I should have been smarter. Better prepared. But how could I when my father had a past I couldn't recall and never imagined even though I'd lived through some small portion of it as a child? Instead I'd gone into this evening with just the rented designer dress on my back, my pricy stilettos and my cell. When Rojas's bodyguard confiscated my phone he effectively stole my transportation options as well, leaving me with one choice. Run. So that's what I was doing.

We'd existed under the weight of unpaid bills for years. Every time we'd almost catch up another treatment or trial would look promising and we'd race to enroll Mama in it, figuring we'd scrounge together money to pay later. We blew through our savings years ago. Even before Mama got sick we hadn't achieved the kind of living standard which could enable us to put aside something for a rainy day...or in this case a monsoon of a cancer diagnosis. So the bills piled up.

But Papá hadn't shared details with me. He never did. He withheld key facts while making unilateral decisions which affected my entire existence. Even though I was a twenty-five-year-old woman with an advanced chemistry degree, I was still a child in his eyes. Which was why I knew nothing about what was truly going on. If he'd explained what was really happening, if he'd disclosed the true circumstances of our fiscal distress, and the life-altering choices he'd made to alleviate it, I still would've showed up tonight to meet our potential benefactor because I was a good daughter.

But then again, maybe I wasn't so good after all. Wouldn't a good daughter be waiting for Rojas in his private suite inside the swanky new westside hotel? Would a good daughter have run away from our supposed financial salvation like I was doing now? Maybe not. But I didn't care anymore. Damn my father's solution.

I was calling the shots now. An arranged marriage was one thing. I could hardly absorb Papá's words when he begged me to meet someone he referred to as an old work contact, a successful businessman. Bad enough I was seriously contemplating a loveless, bloodless union—exchanging myself for the money to cover our debt. But once I realized who Reinaldo Rojas really was, once he pawed me in that humiliating manner even though we were surrounded by dozens of people, it took no imagination to figure out what he'd do once we were alone in his suite. Something snapped when I realized who he was. And showing up in his suite like a lamb to slaughter was not happening.

Rojas's bodyguard, Pablo, requested my phone when I arrived, a security precaution he said, and yes, I already told you I was gullible. Apprehension hit me square between the shoulder blades as I entered the lavishly decorated ballroom without my device. God knows, back in the day I'd fought long and hard with my old-fashioned parents for the ability to carry a cell phone in the first place. But I reasoned what he'd asked was a commonplace enough request where privacy was prized and paparazzi lurked everywhere. Didn't royalty and A-list celebrities confiscate cell phones even from invited guests at their wedding celebrations?

Still, as I listened to the conversations around me, it was clear no paparazzi were in the room. This was one hundred percent Rojas's secure, invitation-only party—not a ticketed event. No one attended this reception who hadn't been expressly invited by Rojas himself. To be brutally honest, Pablo hadn't *asked* to hold my phone. He'd yanked the cell from my perspiring grip without my agreement and I'd been taken so off guard, I hadn't uttered a word of protest. Maybe I'd been too busy reveling in the glamorous crowd, maybe I was wowed by the jewelry and the overwhelming vibe screaming *wealth and class* which emanated from every single person there. And maybe overriding it all, had been my unshakeable conviction, before tonight, that my father never would've condoned this evening's meeting if this important man he set me up with was not to be trusted. I told you I was naïve.

Thankfully the scattered clumps of people— mingling in the gilded, marble and mahogany ballroom, their excited chatter amping louder as their conversations competed with the piped in music, a combination of techno and cumbia— distracted Rojas. When I excused myself to use the restroom, his body guard trailed behind me into the corridor outside the ballroom, and my absence caused barely a ripple of notice.

Outside the ballroom, I continued my fake-casual stroll towards the ladies room even after Rojas's handler turned his back on me. But outside the restroom door, instinct told me to quicken my pace down the darkened, carpeted passageway leading to the hotel's side lobby at Thirty-Fifth Street. If I was going to get out of there, I'd never get a better chance. I strode as fast as I could toward the avenue or at least as fast as my five inch heels would allow, scanning the street for a taxi. But the taxis shooting past me were all occupied and without a phone to call a car service, I had no option but to run. With a stiletto in each hand, I took off.

And thank you high school track, once I got going, I moved on autopilot. Going over the sparse information my father divulged, I wondered how I could've been so ignorant about what tonight was all about. Papá told me I was invited to attend a cocktail party at a chic hotel in a newly gentrified neighborhood on the far westside of Manhattan where a Señor Rojas would be present. I had no idea Rojas organized the evening, no idea who he really was. I agreed to go to the party, which he described as a spring celebration attended by some well-connected New Yorkers and numerous Colombians visiting the city over the Easter season— simply *to meet Rojas.*

Was I so shallow I'd allowed the opportunity to wear an elegant cocktail dress blind me to the reality my desperate parent arranged for me tonight? And how could I have disregarded years of self-defense training, simply because I reasoned I was mingling with a fashionable, upscale crowd— not dancing in some downtown club. Not that I'd ever gone clubbing except that one never to be forgotten, disastrous time in high school with Ivy. I could almost smile at my high school antics, at the self who wanted so badly to do what she thought the other kids got away with. But we hadn't gotten away with it once Ivy's brother Shane found out and came to get us.

Anyway the point being I had no high-pitched, antimugging whistle, or a jacked-up key ring on me tonight—no protection of any kind. Goosebumps chilled and tightened the skin of my arms at the recollection of the waking nightmare of the long minutes inside the small ballroom where I was surrounded by scores of people yet utterly alone and defenseless.

Had Papá known Reinaldo Rojas would paw at me like I was animal in front of an entire ballroom of people? Had he cared? Or had he been so eager to be rid of our great burden, the weight of the debt he'd accrued, he'd been ready to sacrifice me to a revolting excuse for a man? I wouldn't let my mind go there. Not yet. All I knew was, I wasn't going back to that hotel or anywhere near wherever Reinaldo Rojas was. And since there was no other way for us to get out from under our debt, we'd leave the city. We were out of options.

By now, Rojas would be reacting to my absence. It was obvious no one, especially not a mere woman, left his presence without his permission. Hadn't Pablo told me to go immediately to the private suite off the ballroom after I used the restroom? Hadn't he told me not to dare keep the señor waiting? Rojas's bodyguard flaunted the gun in his jacket as he walked me toward the restroom and that's when I knew. He might've thought the sight of a weapon would convince me to stay. But that's when I decided getting out of there was my only choice. Pablo wouldn't have strayed far from the restroom area. I grabbed my opportunity and literally ran.

Running barefoot in a champagne color silk cocktail dress on city streets might have looked bizarre anywhere else but this was New York City. A spring Saturday night in Manhattan was both bucolic and pulsing with life, the glamorous and the grimy side streets littered with people celebrating something or nothing, reveling in the breezy April evening. Weaving my way among them as I raced south along the Hudson River pathway, I didn't care how I looked to anyone who might notice me.

All I cared about was putting miles between me and the criminal who wanted me in payment for a debt.

I'd be home soon. Papá would be annoyed I left the party after less than an hour with the person I'd gone there to meet, gone there to impress, but I was far beyond simple annoyance. My father had to have known exactly what awaited me in that hotel ballroom tonight. Papá was well aware Rojas wasn't an older, wealthy businessman from our home country looking for a wife. My father couldn't possibly have illusions about the man Rojas was because he'd once worked for him. Reinaldo Rojas wasn't a man who was willing to settle a debt in exchange for the opportunity to meet a young, available woman to marry and damn, that scenario had twisted my stomach so tight I thought nothing could be worse. *Meet Esmeralda Acosta, Ms. Dangerously Naïve, NYC.*

I pushed my tumultuous thoughts aside and put one foot in front of the other. I didn't have time to be angry and I didn't have time to berate myself. *Yet.* I had to get home. We'd pack up and go. And we'd do it fast. Moving on short notice was what we knew. This time the move wouldn't be to find a cheaper place. This time the smart thing to do, the only thing, was to leave the city, the state even, and start over somewhere else. Somewhere big and anonymous. Maybe Texas. I'd finally figured out what we were up against and no one had to tell me defying Reinaldo Rojas was not a health-enhancing life decision.

I pelted as fast as I could southbound along the pedestrian path adjacent to the river. My throat burned and my eyes watered so much with the effort I could barely distinguish the familiar outlines of the southern-most skyscrapers gracing the tip of Manhattan. Eventually the Statue of Liberty, the beautiful beacon in the harbor far beyond the path, signaled I was downtown. Any minute I'd turn east toward our neighborhood. Finally. I was fifteen minutes running distance from our apartment maybe less if I poured it on the way I used to back in the days of track meets. But back then I wasn't dodging traffic— barefoot. Back then I didn't spend my nine to five in a lab coat behind a computer.

The stitch in my right side pinched sharper, its deep twist ordering me to stop and catch my breath. As I approached the corner I slowed, indecision and fatigue wobbling my spine and liquifying my legs. I dragged in a labored breath. No. I couldn't stop. Not till I was home. I'd never forget the deadly look in Reinaldo Rojas's assessing eyes or the invasive touch of his hands on my body. No, I'd never forget. Not even if I lived to be an ancient *abuela* back in Colombia.

Keep going, Esme.

I forced my limbs into forward motion. Only a couple more miles.

"Esme?"

The rough as gravel voice bellowing my name was raw with disbelief. I faltered, my gait unsteady. It took me a second to recognize the voice even though I hadn't heard it in ten years. Even though I never thought I'd hear it again. It was deeper, gruffer than before. And yet somehow, it enveloped me like a warm blanket. Had I collapsed? Was I hallucinating? Probably not because the chill April air blowing in from the river was whipping my hair into my eyes. I swiped a hand across my face to brush it away so I could see, swaying as my numb legs slowed to a stumbling walk.

"Esme!"

It *was* him. Shane. Everything in me stilled. Calmed.

I stopped moving but I couldn't see more than shadows. My vision was disoriented by the glare of the lamp-post I stood under as well as the klieg-type security lights, which stayed lit twenty-four seven in certain parts of the World

Trade Center area. Instinctively, I backed out from under the spotlight of the lamp-post. For all I knew, Rojas's guy was right behind me.

"Esme!" The voice carried the weight of command, the authority to halt me right there at the corner of Liberty and West Streets. Now that I'd finally stopped moving it took effort to remain upright when all I wanted was to sink into the pavement like summer rain on sun-parched earth. I stopped my freefall by bending forward, bracing my palms on my scraped knees, hauling in gasping breaths, feeling the sting of every tiny cut on the bottom of my feet. On top of that my muscles were burning in shocked surprise at my impromptu workout. High school track was almost ten years ago.

Had tonight's traumatic events pushed me into a dream state where my deepest desires became reality? Was I so weak I'd conjured him up out of my pathetic need for comfort and security? Giving in, I turned, hopeful, but not believing. His protective nature and friendly, twinkling eyes had once been everything to me. Everything masculine, everything sexy, quite simply *everything* to fifteen-year-old me. In truth, Shane Joseph Fortunato, eldest child in his big family, meant everything to me from the first time he welcomed me, him a beanpole twelve-year-old boy offering a can of soda to the new kid on the block— the shy, Spanish speaking five year old who moved next door to the boisterous Fortunato family.

"Esme, it *is* you." Deep and incredulous, his voice carried from the passenger seat of a beat up Nissan sedan stopped at the light. In seconds he was out of the car and coming toward me, his loose-limbed stride purposeful. I froze. I couldn't have moved if my life depended on it and man, I hoped it didn't because I'd do anything to stay put, right here, with Shane.

He muttered something over his shoulder to the driver who took off with the light change. Then he stood there, his physique nothing like the lean frame of the twenty-one-year-old Shane I remembered. His bulky, thickly muscled shoulders strained the fabric of his gray tee shirt as he shrugged into a leather jacket and stuffed his big hands into the front pockets of his black jeans.

He stared, shock evident in his unsmiling eyes as he leveled his intense blue gaze on me, his expression severe, critically intent and so different from the laughing Shane of our childhoods. He didn't miss one bit of the grime-streaked, perspiration soaked dress I'd rented, the once sophisticated up-do of my long hair, presently hanging down my back in a sweaty tumble. His hard gaze narrowed on my cut up, grimy feet, scraped knees and elbow before skimming back up to my face. I wanted to laugh at the irony. After all this time, this was so not the way I pictured meeting Shane again. And God help me, I'd pictured our reunion way too many times to count.

But none of that mattered now. I had to keep my focus and keep going.

"Shane." I raised my chin then dropped it down quickly in a nod of acknowledgement, my voice a little breathless from an hour of running but happily quite steady, as if meeting Shane Fortunato on a random city street, after midnight for the first time in ten years—with me, grubby and barefoot, was no big deal.

CHAPTER 2

SHANE

*T*HE WAY she said my name. God. With her barely there accent I knew she wanted to lose and keep in equal measure. Deep down I feared, no, I was sure, I'd never hear the sultry music of her voice again. But Esme was here, right here, only blocks from where I live. If I hadn't been on my way home from my four by twelve shift with my partner Alex, me half-listening while he vented about his toddler son's teething, then debating the merits of the Yankee and Mets seasons, the way we always did—if we hadn't been stopped at this traffic light, I might've missed her. My heart froze then took a woozy dive into my boots at the total randomness of it.

Esme. I was stunned to actually be face to face with her after all this time. Or was my mind playing tricks on me? Wouldn't be the first time. Could be one of those dreams again. Dreams so vivid I could almost inhale the coconut scent that surrounded her when she came by our house especially that last time ten years ago. Esme had starred in my dreams at least weekly since then. Please God, this wasn't a dream. But damn, if it was, it was the weirdest one yet. What was Esme doing running full tilt down the sidewalk in a fairy tale dress of flowing gold after midnight? My heart did that rollercoaster plunge again as I examined the nasty cuts, grit and blood marring her beautiful skin. Nope, this was no dream. More like a nightmare. What in hell happened?

"Esme, what's going on? You're covered in blood."

She bristled at my shouted words and her chin tilted up. "Not covered. I fell." She stood straighter and hiked up one bare shoulder, all casual. Like this scenario wasn't freakin' outrageous. I took a small step toward her, swallowing the urge to argue the point. *Stop. Pay attention to what's going on here. Esme needs help. Attend to her. Then get to the bottom of whatever this craziness is.*

"Okay." I nodded. "You're injured," I said, sticking to facts. I forced my shoulders down, fake-relaxed, smothering thoughts of the past and the future and focusing on the here and now. I tamped my tone down to conversational, flicking my gaze to her strappy heels. "Why aren't you wearing your shoes?"

Her gaze jumped to fix somewhere over my shoulder and I could tell right away she was trying to come up with a whopper I'd believe. Just like she did when she and Ivy went to that club. Sorry, honey. I've heard them all. And if not from my six younger siblings, then certainly from the humanity I deal with on a daily basis.

"Esmeralda." I struggled to keep my tone even. This was the first time I'd seen her in ten years. This was the first time I'd said her name out loud in the same span of time. I wouldn't shout. And I couldn't grab her, pick her up and hold her close to my heart the way I did in my dreams.

"Please." I made the effort and softened my voice. "Tell me. It's after midnight. When I first spotted you, you looked like you were running from the devil himself."

My words prompted a choked cry from her and she

turned sideways but not before I saw her almond shaped eyes fill. Fast as that she lifted a hand to dash the tears away, glaring at me all the while. Straight-backed, she crossed her arms over her chest and cocked her hip.

"Shane! I can't stand here chatting with you. I've got to go…"

When she threw an anxious glance behind her, clammy fear climbed my back to sit heavy on my shoulders and years of training crushed my indecision.

"Let's go." I grasped her hand, urging her into the shadow of one of the maple trees lining this part of the Hudson Riverwalk while I connected to car service. In a minute a car pulled up, courtesy of the city that never sleeps. In spite of her bluster she climbed in after she scanned the street behind her—for what I didn't know. I vowed then I'd do anything to live up to the confidence in me she revealed in that moment.

As the driver shot across town I relaxed enough to turn and look at her. The girl—the woman—I hadn't seen in so long. The face I'd never forgotten and would never forget. The woman I reminded myself daily I might never see again. Stunning and fine boned as ever with liquid green eyes I'd gladly drown in, long glossy hair, skin a shade of warm, luminescent amber I'd never seen on anyone else. The beautiful skin on limbs now raw with welts and scrapes.

The car pulled up at my Church Street address and she peered out the window at the modern ten story residential building, then back at me, a half smile curving her lower lip. I returned her look lifting my brow.

"What?" I asked.

"We live about two miles east of here."

"That's insane." We grinned like loons at each other at the strange coincidence of it. And even though I could've gotten drunk on Esme's big smile, underneath my smile was the knowledge she'd been here, practically on my doorstep and I didn't know. It twisted something in my gut. How could Esme be living in lower Manhattan and I didn't know? I'd convinced myself she'd moved out of the city. When I became a cop, I'd done some discreet checking and found an address. But when that location turned out to be vacant I forced myself to stop because I'm not a stalker. If Esme left the old neighborhood without telling anyone her forwarding address, it was her business— a decision I had to respect. But it never stopped me wondering how she was, where she was, what she might be doing. Right now, I could hardly believe we were breathing the same air.

"How long?" I asked.

"Almost a year now." She shrugged and her smile faded as she pressed her lush lips into a straight line.

"We?" I had no business asking her in a voice I couldn't stop from sounding clipped but I had to know. I'd forced myself to acknowledge long ago I was no one special to Esme. Yes, we'd been neighbors, she'd spent a lot of time in our house when we were kids but that was a long time ago. I hadn't set eyes on her since she was nearly sixteen and I was twenty-one. Ten years had passed. Whoever she lived with was one hundred and ten percent her business. But damn, whoever he was, he was doing a piss poor job of looking out for her.

"Your husband?" I spat out the words like a curse.

"Oh. No. My father. I live with my father." She tilted her head sideways as she said it, examining me with curious eyes. That's when I remembered I used to call her little bird when she'd first moved on to our block. She'd perch on the railing in front of our building, quietly observant as all of us, my younger siblings and me, wandered home from school. Her mother, Gloria was usually home because she taught piano and voice from the front room of their apartment. Esme came outside after speeding through her homework, leaving her mother to tend to the gaggle of hapless students waiting for lessons in their living room. Smart cookie that she always was, school was easy for her, even more amazing when you factored in that when she first moved to the states, the only word of English she knew was Fanta. Since she had no siblings, no doubt the Fortunato kids provided Esme with a bottomless well of cheap entertainment over the years we'd lived in side by side tenements.

The breath I let out was half laugh, half groan. "So, you're not married...?" The reality was unbelievable and my chest expanded and contracted so violently I rubbed a hand over my heart. I always knew I wasn't good enough for Esme. Besides she was too young for me. But damn, even at fifteen she'd been the full package—whip smart, full of sparkle and drop-dead gorgeous. All in all, a person destined for great things. In my darkest moments in the service and after Christopher, I had the comfort of the certainty she was living like the princess she always deserved to be.

"No," she answered solemnly, "not yet."

Not yet? What the fuck did that mean? "So what exactly is going on?" I asked with all the patience I could muster.

CHAPTER 3

ESME

*H*OW COULD I encapsulate any of these last years, never mind what happened tonight to Shane without sounding like a tragic heroine in a telenovela? I wasn't married, no. But if I didn't do something about it, and Reinaldo Rojas had his way, I could be tied to him in marriage or some other way of his choosing, all with my father's blessing. My father had skillfully led me down a path of half-truths and evasions, counting on me to perceive the rationale for what he was doing. The reasons behind his twisted arrangements. And because I'd run out on Rojas, reality was whatever arrangement he'd made with my father could be the lesser evil I faced because there was a very real chance a furious Rojas would come after us. And not to talk about an arranged marriage. He could decide the stupid girl who had the nerve to leave his exalted presence and her hapless father didn't deserve to live. How had we gotten to such a sorry place?

I hadn't paid enough attention. I'd poured my sorrow at Mama's death into my work as a medical researcher. My job was all consuming and I welcomed the single-minded focus I lavished on my career, especially these last several months. Grief pushed me to submerse myself in lab studies and trials inching toward the next breakthrough treatment. Being a tiny cog in a huge research machine hunting for a cure was my reason to get up in the morning. That and making sure my father was okay.

But it wasn't the same for my father. With every year that passed his construction laborer's job stole more of his strength. His emotional reserves and his joy in life completely vanished when Mama passed. Our six-thirty dinners took place in near silence. Whenever I treated myself to an occasional evening meal with a friend, he usually didn't eat at all, so gradually I declined those invitations. Daily conversation consisted solely of basic questions about groceries or laundry—or was non-existent. The only good thing about his job was the utterly exhausted sleep he fell into every night, ever more frequently with an assist from alcohol. Now Mama was gone, my father was mentally one step in the grave. We lived together but Papá and I existed in solitary worlds of grief.

It came back to Mama. Neither of us had recovered from her death. The field I worked in today was a daily reminder of her struggle to defeat the blood cancer which took her life. We grieved her still, but more than that, we'd gotten ourselves into an insurmountable financial hole paying for treatment after treatment and searching high and low for the best care available. Knowing our debts remained unpaid only served to prolong our mourning.

The three of us were in shock after Mama's diagnosis. Mama's symptoms began when I was a rising junior in high school. In one fell swoop everything changed—even though Mama fought hard to maintain our version of normal life and at first worked during and between her chemo treatments.

Forced to react to a new and increasingly dire set of circumstances every few months, it didn't occur to me to wonder how we would pay for the care Mama received. But I should have wondered. Because Papá's non-union, laborer's job and Mama's income as a neighborhood music teacher were never up to the task of saving for a rainy day much less a cancer diagnosis. And back when Mama first got sick, I was years away from being able to assist financially. *But I should have known. I should have figured it out.* As I got older and bills piled up, I accepted we'd have enormous debt. I began to pay for groceries and as much of my mother's medical costs as I could manage while my father paid the rent.

It was hard to remember a time when Papá and I hadn't been lost and exhausted on the hamster wheel of getting Mama whatever she needed. We always hoped the next treatment or the next one would work, searching out one new trial after another. Eventually our money was spent not on treatments but the best home health aide, and finally the comfort of home hospice to ease Mama's last days.

When we'd come to this country twenty years ago, Papá actively rejected his connections to the drug trade which, once upon a time in Colombia, transformed him from a struggling farmer into a financially stable, if not wealthy, courier. We'd started a new life here in the states, giving our landlord my mother's surname, Acosta. I'd only been going on six-years-old when we arrived here, and I never quite pieced together the details my parents sought to keep hidden. And I still hadn't gotten the full story. Until tonight.

Although I'd kept Acosta as my surname through graduations and jobs, every time we moved including this last time after Mama passed, to our sixth, smallest, and cheapest apartment, I heard Papá giving the landlord yet another fictitious surname. By this time I assumed Papá was dodging debt collectors and that was true—though not in the way I imagined. It was obvious now. Fake names and frequent moves hadn't made a difference. Those subterfuges hadn't kept us off Reinaldo Rojas's radar.

WHEN PAPÁ PULLED me aside a few weeks ago, when he told me about tonight's event, I was stunned and even then I didn't have the complete picture. Bad enough he was trying to marry me off for money to pay bills. I still remember my pure shock that night as I stood at the stove making another cheap, carbo-loaded meal both of us would only pick at. How I listened to his stilted speech in increasing horror as he sought to convince me an advantageous union to an influential businessman would erase the debt he had no other way of paying.

"Married? No way, Papá. That's crazy. I have a decent job," I argued. Not a fantastic salary but I was climbing the ladder at a major New York City research hospital and I had benefits. "Let's think this through. I'm sure there's a way we can pay down our debt monthly."

But he only shook his head and gazed at me with blank, defeated eyes before he explained slowly, treating me, as always, like a child. "We were given a loan...but not from a bank. The interest payments alone are beyond anything we could ever hope to repay."

"A loan shark? Is that what you mean? You got money from a loan shark? Papá, how? Why didn't you tell me? I wish you'd told me." Regret consumed me when I thought about the stupid, frivolous excesses I'd spoiled myself with over the years, not much in themselves but nothing I should have cared about. I took his arm, tried to look into his eyes but he turned away, choosing to stare out the unadorned, front window of our apartment. People were returning home from work and the drivers of the cars creeping along Eldridge Street were all looking for parking.

Still not looking at me, speaking almost to himself, Papá said, "This is not what I wanted, Esmeralda. Believe me, this is not what I planned. But when the time came, when we needed that money, I had no other choice. He was there when I needed help. He appeared almost like the answer to a prayer. So I took the loan. What alternative did I have? None. There was nothing else I could do. No one else could help us. But *m'ija*, I have no regrets. I would have done anything, I *did* do anything I could to find a treatment, a cure, then… anything to ease your mother's last days. It was the only way I could do my best for her. The only way I could give her a chance."

He turned to me finally, and grasped my hands. "Por favor, go. Meet Señor Rojas. You never know. You may decide… he…he is the one for you."

And wasn't it strange, when Papá said those words, *the one for you*, only one face popped into my mind? The one for me? There had only ever been one person for me even though I never shared the adolescent crush I'd never managed to outgrow with anyone except his brother Christopher. The one for me had always been Shane Fortunato.

But Papá made his point. The piper had to be paid. With every illusion about my father stripped away, I had a front row seat on a world which had been kept hidden from me for years. I was certainly not a child now. Not anymore. Tonight I realized *I* was the payment. Tonight, I found out Reinaldo Rojas wasn't an influential businessman who doled out charitable loans to his Colombian countrymen and God help me for being so damned foolish, but I wanted to believe something different. Something less vile than the truth. Reinaldo Rojas was the head of one of the most powerful cocaine cartels in South America, maybe the world. My father had worked for him when we still lived in Colombia and on the strength of their prior relationship, Rojas made my father a significant loan when we were desperate to pay medical bills, anxious to help Mama survive. I knew nothing of it. I knew nothing about his connection to my father back when we lived in Colombia and apparently, I didn't need to know. I was just the daughter. A child. Now I'm a woman who is a pawn. Unless I could figure a way out.

CHAPTER 4

SHANE

*E*SME WASN'T TALKING but she fidgeted plenty as she avoided answering my basic question. It didn't make me a genius to know something was up. Something serious enough she'd been racing barefoot down the city streets at midnight. Running from…what?

Part of me wanted to comfort her, assure her everything would be okay. The other part of me needed to find out what was going on so I could fix it—take that haunted look out of her eyes. I decided I would do both. Comfort her and fix it.

I could tell she was wary but she took my hand and allowed me to help her from the car. That alone made me feel like a king. She trusted me. I resisted the urge to lift her fully into my arms to spare her poor, mangled feet for two reasons. One, I may have teased her about being skinny as a bird when she was a kid. But there was nothing birdlike about her now. The tensile strength shaping her arms and her long lean legs showed she was still the athlete, the runner she'd been in high school even if she was an injured one right now. She would want to walk on her own two feet.

Second, Esme was a knockout. She was going to be noticed no matter what. But if the guy at the front desk saw me carry her, it would draw attention to her scrapes and cuts and the fact that her shoes were dangling from my pocket. He could pass that information on to interested parties. I couldn't allow that to happen when I didn't even know who the interested parties were.

"Sergeant." The overnight guy behind the desk was new and clearly untrained because he wasn't even trying to disguise his open perusal of Esme. I issued him a curt nod. Though not often, I'd brought a woman back to my place on occasion. But I could do without the knowing glance this kid bestowed on us, could do without his not so-surreptitious examination of Esme. Her eyes darted behind me to the door as we moved beyond the lobby's front desk. I could feel her willing me to move faster toward the elevator bank.

Nothin' to see here, sport, my body language said to the desk guy. Under my fixed stare he finally lowered his eyes to the security screen on his counter.

Instinct kept me shielding Esme with my body as we continued across the empty lobby toward the elevator, though I had no clue what I was protecting her from. But protect her I would. My building was one of those renovated in the aftermath of 9/11 and the lobby impressed, with its cool black granite floor and display of enormous modern photographs of metropolitan skylines from around the world. It exuded a serene vibe and most important, came with top-notch security—new guy, numb-nuts at the front desk notwithstanding.

My apartment was the best I could afford on my NYPD salary: modern, compact and functional. A far cry from the tenement of my childhood even though I surprised myself sometimes wishing I was back in Hell's Kitchen. Not strange when I thought about it because in those days both Esme and

Christopher were near me all the time. But now Esme was here with me at last though under the strangest circumstances. And Christopher, well, I carried him in my heart.

When the doors opened on the seventh floor the breath she eased out tickled my chin. Her tense shoulders drooped as we walked down the thick, silver gray carpet to my corner apartment. I keyed open both locks and the deadbolt, thankful for once as the oldest of seven I'd absorbed all of Ma's persnickety rules about keeping tidy as I went, as she would say. There might be a coffee mug in the sink but my bed was made and the bathroom had clean towels because today was Saturday and I'd done laundry before my shift. I threw my keys onto the short oak dresser that served as a front hall table and waved an encompassing hand at the open floor plan space with its polished, engineered oak wood floors.

"Welcome to my small slice of paradise," I said with a twist to my lips. I stored my weapon in the locked bottom drawer of the same dresser, ducking my chin so I wouldn't see her expression at her first look at my basic living space. The dress she wore was probably silk, but whatever it was, it looked expensive with sequins and tiny pearls lining the neckline, and the high heels in my pocket boasted red soles. I'd seen plenty of the kind of clothes and shoes my sister Holly loved to wear to know. By all the evidence Esme was living the good life right now. Which begged the question—what was she running from?

Her half smile turned distant as she crossed the living area to peer out the windows. Behind her the lights of the city both man made and real, winked and glowed and I'm amazed I even had that thought because usually I pulled the shade on the harsh illumination that flooded my apartment some nights. *That was Esme.* Even bedraggled and injured, she brought it. She sparkled enough to fool the garish city lights into looking like precious gems. But even in the city the night would win, if only for a little while. Before long, inky black would temporarily swallow the silver sky. The city wouldn't sleep, though. Sometimes it only took a cat nap. And me, a cop, knew that better than most. Esme turned to look as I came up behind her and there was that smile again. The same shy curve of lush lips I thought I'd never see again.

"I like it." She nodded approvingly at the quartz countertops and stainless appliances in the compact kitchen. "It's cool. Modern. You've come a long way from Forty-Sixth Street, Shane."

Damn, I could feel my face heat. What was it about Esme? From the first moment I met her and apparently still to this day I was a blithering idiot in her presence. I had to keep reminding myself she was a friend I hadn't seen in long years. A friend who needed help.

"Sit down…anywhere. I'll get you something to drink."

"Shane. I can't be here. I've got to get home," she said, her hands tight fists at her side.

"C'mon, Esme, just a couple of minutes and I'll take you wherever you need to go. You've gotta be thirsty." *And I've gotta find out why you look like an injured Cinderella.*

"And you are bossy as ever," she said. With a toss of her head she sat though, and in spite of her skinned knees and scraped feet she looked like a princess perched on the edge of the gray couch situated so one could see both the downtown view and the television.

I grabbed a cold one from the fridge for me and pulled out a Fanta for her.

"Shane! Fanta?" Her anxious look disappeared and her grin burst open, big, joyous and all I could think of was the explosion of sunflowers Mom grew in her garden at Rockaway every summer. "Who else do you know likes Fanta?"

She took the can from me with a raised brow, curiosity brightening her green eyes.

I stayed silent so long it felt weird. It *was* weird. I kept a six pack of Fanta around for her. For Esme. I'd been doing it for literal years, periodically drinking them and replacing them. Yeah, I told you it was weird.

I shrugged. "I like Fanta, too."

The wing of her raven dark eyebrow elevated higher as she pointedly gazed at my half-finished beer. "Most of the time," I amended. *Change the subject before she figures out you drink them on her birthday, on the holidays and other random days when you've awakened from a dream of her and just want to feel close. Hell.*

I angled my chin at her knees, peeping out from under the silk of her dress. "What's going on, Esme? How'd you get hurt?"

Now it was her turn to clam up. She took a long pull on her soda. I almost forgot how much I loved how her eyelids fluttered shut as she sipped. My gaze tracked the smooth skin of her throat as she swallowed slow then wiped her mouth with the back of her hand. I waited for her to speak, reveling, after so long, in the exquisite pleasure of her presence. Besides, in my work I'd learned the value of patience. So few detectives ever mastered simple observation and watchful waiting.

She opened her mouth then closed it again shifting minutely in her seat. I placed a careful hand on her left knee. We both looked down at the sticky, dark-red, congealed blood near my fingers. The sight of the blood broke her silence and she blurted. "Can I borrow your phone? I have to call my father." I pulled my phone from my pocket and handed it to her, incapable of denying her anything. Was it possible in this day and age she still didn't own a cell phone? No. But I didn't see a purse either. She must've been robbed. Some piece of crap had ripped Esme off. That's why she was running. But why had she been alone? "Make your call. I'll get some first aid stuff to clean this all up." I waved a hand at her knees, shocked and embarrassed to sense my own knees weakening at the sight of the rusty blood and livid cuts marring her skin. That was another *only with Esme* feeling. I could always steel myself no matter what the situation to take care of business first and shut off emotional response till the danger passed. I mean, I've been in war zones. I've arrested some pretty fucked up characters. But I couldn't turn off my emotional response with Esme. Never could. I remembered grabbing her and Ivy out of that sleazy club back when they were teenagers. I'd been angry as hell they finagled their way in there to begin with but when I saw them standing together on the long line waiting for the bar, my knees went wobbly with relief.

When I returned with a washcloth, peroxide, gauze, and Band-aids, she clicked off the cell and laid it beside her on the sofa. Then she picked up the enormous seashell on the end table, the one I found on the Rockaway shore. Big as a boot, it was a size you never saw around there anymore. She cradled it in her lap and started tracing the edges of it, one slender pink painted nail running along the edges of it over and over. Her graceful movements couldn't disguise the tense set of her shoulders.

"Did you reach your dad?"

She glanced up at me with blank eyes, unable to pull herself back from wherever her thoughts went. My cop sense sparked all over again at her shuttered expression. "Yes. We spoke. Shane, I have to go. My father...I have to go." She started to stand but I stayed her with a hand to her elbow.

"Yeah, sure. I'll take you home. Let's get these cuts cleaned up. But c'mon, Esme, you can't really think I'm gonna let you go without telling me what happened tonight. I want to help. No matter what it is I *can* help you. Trust me."

She twisted her lower lip with her teeth and clammed up again. I forced my focus to the matter at hand because let's face it, the more I pushed the more she shut down. Tonight we'd met up with each other for the first time in ten years, so why should she tell me anything? Yet I wanted, *I needed* for her to confide in me what in hell happened to her tonight. It wasn't so weird, was it? It's what a friend would do, right? Had she done something illegal? If so, I was the last person she'd wanna tell. In seconds the unsettling realization hit me. Cop or not, no matter what she'd done, I'd never rat her out. But it didn't matter because the concept of Esme committing a crime was ludicrous. I'd never met a straighter arrow, a kid more likely to succeed no matter what you put her up against.

"This might hurt but I'll be gentle," I promised. Her lips tightened a fraction but Esme was stoic as I dabbed at the wounds with successive pieces of peroxide dampened gauze, carefully removing the grit and dirt from the nasty scrapes. After her initial wince at the cold sting of the peroxide she held still as a statue, as I covered the first knee with two large Band-Aids before working on the other.

"You're pretty good at this." Her words puffed out in a soft rush of breath.

I looked up from her knee to see if she was teasing. The gleam in her eye said she was.

Shrugging, with one corner of my mouth ticking upwards into a half smile, I refocused on my task. "And you remember why. I've lost count of the times I was designated medic when one of my siblings fell off a bike or got busted up in a fight." I fixed a new bandage to her other knee with gentle pressure.

She presented her elbow before she responded, her voice

barely above a whisper. "I remember. I remember everything."

All of the sudden we were back ten years ago at my going away party right before I entered the service with Esme smiling her serious smile as she ordered me not to forget her and me telling her there was no chance it would ever happen. We'd been next door neighbors, friends, nothing more, even though when I got older, I'd endured long, restless nights thinking about her and wishing we were closer in age. I hadn't forgotten her. Not for a single day since.

Still, I hadn't lived like a monk. I'd had a couple of long-term girlfriends over the ten years since I'd last seen Esme. One relationship lasted for the better part of two years. But the mind was a weird thing, or at least mine was freakin' impossible to fathom. As the years passed, even though I told myself I'd never see Esme again—I also hadn't been able, at now thirty-two years old, to seal the deal on any other relationship. I usually broke things off before expectations of permanency set in. Because something was missing. Because no matter how perfect a woman seemed on paper, none of them was Esme. Then there was the cop factor. In my last relationship a year ago, Lori broke it off first. She gave me an ultimatum about quitting the force. She wasn't cut out to be a cop's wife, she said. She didn't even want to be a cop's girlfriend. So yeah, there was that.

Esme leaned toward me, sucking in a quick breath as I swabbed the last of the grit off her elbow. Her scent, coconut mixed with the earthier, saltiness of sweat, washed over me. "One thing I always wondered Shane, who bandaged you when you got hurt?" Her voice had the quality of music to my Esme-starved ears, muted and melodious. It weakened and strengthened me at the same time. No surprise. From the very first, Esme had tied me up in knots. I could feel her keen gaze boring into my profile but I kept my focus on her torn up elbow.

I lifted a shoulder. "I was invincible."

"Was?" Her voice was teasing, curious. *She didn't know about Christopher.*

I rubbed my free hand over the scruff on my chin. "I grew up. Had to...accept certain things. Y'know?"

"Yeah, I know the feeling." Her gaze skidded back up to mine. "Tonight I met a man my father arranged for me to marry."

My fingers fumbled at the broken skin of her elbow but I managed a nod for her to continue, not trusting my voice. Okay, so she was ready to tell me what went down tonight, how she got these injuries. What in hell did it have to do with getting married? *And what the fuck, karma?* Had I finally met Esme again only to see her marry someone else?

"My father asked me to meet him. He told me I was meeting," she swallowed, "a...successful man and ...if I married him, he'd give us the money to pay our debts." She swallowed again and when her voice emerged it was low and husky. "But tonight when I..."

Dread swept through me like an army of red ants. She faltered over a recounting that was getting more bizarre by the second, choosing her words with care, with long pauses to keep her voice even and her emotions in check. I wanted to interrupt to ask what in hell her father had done but I'd been asking her tell me and now she was talking. I waited a couple of beats after she paused. Esme didn't have to worry anymore. She had me to help now. Once she told me, I'd fix it. I'd destroy whoever was responsible for the trauma she experienced tonight—because I now recognized she was in shock.

"Esme." My hard-learned patience was fast evaporating. What was she saying? Marrying some guy to pay a debt? "Tell me what happened, Esme. Whatever it is, I can help you. I promise, babe." I finally finished with her last scrape and stuck a Band-aid on her elbow.

She dropped her gaze from mine to focus again on the seashell on her lap, tracing the creamy pink interior with her forefinger. I counted the five long breaths she took before she lifted her head and looked me straight in the eye.

"The debts from Mama's care. My mother died the end of last year. But before she did, we spent every cent we had trying to find a treatment, a cure, or just something to make her feel better."

"Oh, babe. I'm so sorry." I covered her cold hands with mine. "I knew she was sick but then by the time I got out of the service you'd moved away. I hoped…" When it came to Esme, I'd hoped so many things. That she'd be happy. Safe. Secure. Looks like life had taken a heartbreaking turn for all of us in the months after I enlisted.

"Yeah, I know. We…, my father and I, kept hoping too." She looked at me and her mesmerizing eyes were completely black, the pupils totally swallowing up the vibrant green for which she was named. She took another long pull from her soda then cleared her throat.

"So I went to the Powell tonight, you know the new hotel on Thirty-Fifth?"

"Yep," I nodded for her to continue and she turned away slightly, like she didn't want my gaze on her face while she spoke. I settled into the other corner of the couch forcing my shoulders to relax.

"I rented this dress." She waved a hand at herself. "To make a good impression."

My stomach clenched. I didn't like the idea of Esme dressing up unless it was her choice. Esme made a good impression on the world just by breathing among the rest of us.

"There were a lot of people there: Americans, South Americans, maybe forty in all. It was showy, lots of jewelry and loud music. The man I was to meet wasn't there at first. But his...I don't know, bodyguard, met me at the door and stuck close. I didn't know a soul there and he was like, glued to me, listening when I spoke to people. Or when they spoke to me. They were all welcoming enough. I mingled, chatting about how hot this spring's been, new exhibits at the Met. I recognized the weather guy from Channel 11 and that retired pitcher from the Mets."

"Wow, Valdez?" Impressive array of people.

With only a hint of a smile for my long time baseball hero-worship, she lifted her shoulders and dropped them, her focus back on the seashell.

I could picture her at the hotel tonight, elegant in her gold dress with all that Convent of the Sacred Heart poise front and center. When she started there on a partial scholarship, she told me she really liked the convent school because everyone wore the same uniform and I totally got that. Uniforms turned out to be a great equalizer and a blessing for kids like us without extra money to spare for trendy clothing. I remember wearing last year's sneakers to public school, all of us in our family did. It sucked. Bullies loved to hone in on that kind of shit. Esme's parents sacrificed to send her to the convent and she was an only. With our big family private school was way out of bounds. And look where the big shot college had gotten Christopher. Tonight, no doubt in my mind, every man at that event, no, every person there, had been floored by Esme's gifts of intellect and beauty.

"Out of the corner of my eye I saw someone step into the room. A middle-aged man, middle height, middle everything and yet I knew. He walked in slowly so everyone would notice, preening like the puffbirds I used to see in Colombia.

He acted like he owned the place and for all I know he does. Anyway I knew by the way everybody there kowtowed to him, practically kissing his ring...he was *somebody*." She shook her head slightly. "Then the guy who was shadowing me, his bodyguard, introduced me to the señor."

CHAPTER 5

ESME

C'MON, Esme stop staring at a seashell like it's going to do your talking for you.

I swallowed, pushing down my anxiety at revealing everything that happened tonight, my fury at my father, the disgust that still permeated every pore of my body. I took another sip of soda. Shane's eyes were calm, his body language deceptively relaxed across from me. His total focus on me should have made me nervous but I reveled in it. God, I'd missed him so much. His patience cloaked me in warmth, his regular slow inhales and exhales, soothed me. I laid the seashell back on the table and reached for his hand, needing his comfort. His capable, callused hand immediately enclosed mine, and then he caught my other hand in his. Safe.

"I think what really got to me was that no one said a thing. These glamorous people, all of them so put together and successful, some of them must've seen what he was doing right in front of them in that fancy ballroom. But not one of them said a word. Not one." I cringed anew at my naivety.

"Saw what, Esme?" Shane's gruff voice was tense.

"What he did. How he touched me." I dropped my gaze to our clasped hands as he tightened his, then raised my chin again and looked him in the eye. His probing-cop gaze trained on me, he nodded minutely.

"He didn't even introduce himself." My hollow laugh was an acknowledgement of just how gullible, no scratch that, how dumb I was. But, God knows, I wasn't anymore. "He didn't shake my hand so much as grab it. He yanked me toward him and I stumbled. I was taller than him in my heels so when he pulled me, I fell toward him, boobs first, crashing into his face. He laughed so loud. Everybody looked at us and then turned away. I was off balance and so close there was less than an inch between us. That was when he gripped my wrist tighter and pressed it backwards."

Shane's rigid body language said he was having a tough time hearing this and yeah, it was difficult to recount. Sure enough when I looked at my wrist there were reddish, finger shaped marks there from Rojas's grip. Shane saw them too and smoothed his thumb over the discolored skin. I cleared my throat again knowing I needed to force out the whole story at once if I was going to get it out at all. "While he was twisting my wrist with one hand...with the other he... touched me, squeezed me—my chin, my neck, my breasts... everywhere... like I was, like I was." I shook my head in self-disgust. *Why hadn't I pulled away?* "I wouldn't even touch an animal like that." I had to finish. "He said...quite loudly," I closed my eyes at the recollection. "He said he was promised a virgin and that was what he'd better get." Shane stiffened but kept rubbing his thumbs over my wrists, and the rhythmic motion calmed me. My eyes filled with angry, humiliated tears but I blinked them away clearing my throat for the millionth time.

"When his hand went under the hem of my dress, I yanked away from him." *Why hadn't I gotten away sooner?* "I thought I was going to puke but I managed a smile and told him I needed the restroom. The señor nodded and let go of me. He told his bodyguard to bring me to his suite after I used the bathroom. *"Inmediatamente,"* he said. When his handler escorted me to the corridor, he made sure I saw his gun."

"The hem of your dress? His gun?" Shane's voice was thunder. I kept speaking. I had to get it all out.

"The other guy, Pablo, shooed me toward the restroom and when he turned back toward the ballroom, I walked past the restroom, out of the hotel and started running. I just... ran. And kept running. That's when you saw me."

"Those cuts and scrapes. How did...?"

"I tripped on a curb when I was running." My run from Rojas was taking on a surreal, nightmarish quality. I could hardly believe I was here with Shane. And safe—for the time being anyway.

He blew out several short breaths, the tee shirt covering his broad chest stretching with each rapid inflate and deflate. Then he dropped my hands to drive his fingers through his already unruly hair. "Esme who in holy hell was this wrong dude? Tell me you know his name because I'm gonna find him and make him wish he never laid a finger on you."

"I know who he is. *Now.* His name is Reinaldo Rojas." As his thick brows rose to his hairline, I said. "Yeah, *that* Reinaldo Rojas."

"What!" Shane's voice exploded as he erupted from his place on the couch. "What were you doing with Reinaldo fuckin' Rojas?"

I shot to my feet. So Shane was upset? Hello, so was I. My hands flew wide and my voice strengthened with every word I uttered. "Do you actually think I possessed a single clue who I was meeting tonight?"

He loosed a wild laugh. "Fuck's sake, Esme. No. No.

'Course not. Sorry. I'm just…this whole thing…" He started pacing, the heels of his boots fast and rhythmic against the glossy floor. He strode the length of the gray couch, past the fancy, sound proofed windows looking out onto Church Street, the force of his anger rolling off of him in furious waves.

"Shane. There's…something else." I waited till Shane stopped pacing and turned toward me but when he did I found I couldn't look him in the eye. He didn't say a word just waited till I could find my own. "Rojas said,"…and man, out of everything that happened this was the part that killed me, just completely gutted me. "He said my father had to know this would happen, that debts to Rojas must always be paid." When I asked how my father would know such a thing he said my father worked for him. Back before we came to the states. I never knew."

Saying it was humiliating enough and not because of anything Shane might think. Because twenty years later I had neither figured it out nor had my father told me the truth. I'd like to think if I'd known we wouldn't be in this mess. But to Rojas and man, it hurt to even think it, to my father too, I was nothing more than a living, breathing reimbursement on a loan. It was as simple and sleazy as that.

Our gazes locked and as I watched, color darkened his cheekbones. My emotions were all over the place but over-riding everything was a deep gratitude fate had brought us together again.

"Esme. I'm sorry for what happened. I know it was rough for you to tell me about it, and horrible to go through in the first place. But it's so… freakin' tough for me to take in. I thought you met a skeevy jerk, that you'd been robbed which was bad enough." He started pacing again. "But no, this perv is also one of the most notorious drug lords in the world. He's in New York, and your dad, *your father* sets you up with

38

him like it's some kind of Tinder date? And the bastard puts hands on you?" He stopped in front of me, cupped my shoulders and lowered his head till his forehead touched mine. "I'm so glad you bolted, babe. It was a freakin' brave thing to do. I'm so damn glad you're here. With me."

"Same." I didn't feel brave. Dumb and naïve were the words foremost in my mind. I believed—because my father told me—I was going to a party to meet a wealthy contact of Papá's. If we were both amenable to marriage, the man would cover the loan we took to pay medical bills. A kind of reverse dowry. When I agreed to meet him the look of relief on my father's face almost made the decision worth it. Almost. Then tonight after five minutes in Rojas's orbit and after Rojas himself told me what was really going on, I acted on instinct and shock. I was *not* brave. I didn't lift my head for long moments. Shane's chest rose and fell with the rapid thump of his heart and then he put his hands to my elbows and stepped back.

"Okay. I need your address. And a recent photo of your Dad." Shane was back in cop mode. "My squad will arrange for surveillance at your place."

He tapped the info into his smart phone as I gave our lower east side address. "But Papá's not there now. When I called him, I told my father I left the event. Alone. He was with a friend. I told him to stay with the friend tonight. After I yelled at him for setting this whole thing up in the first place."

"Damn straight. Okay. Give me the friend's address, too." Shane looked up from his phone, his brows squeezed together so tight there was a deep groove between them.

Embarrassment tightened my throat. Which was ridiculous given everything else about my father Shane already knew. Apparently my father had some measure of guilt about tonight. Not enough to prevent him from sending me straight into the lion's den. But after I left he must've gone right over to the bar a few blocks from our place where he proceeded to get hammered. He was barely coherent when I spoke to him a few minutes ago but I made him promise me —twice, he'd stay with Patricio. "My father was in a bar with a friend of his, a guy named Patricio. He was wasted. Definitely not in the condition to do go home. I told him to stay with Patricio until he heard from me." After I gave him Patricio's address, I closed my eyes and rubbed my chilled arms, but the horrible mashup of tonight's events still scrolled across my mind.

"Okay, good." Shane was all business. "We'll get our people to watch both locations." Then he did what I'd craved from the moment I saw him again. Shane took me fully into his embrace, his protective arms rock-hard around me, his chin resting on the crown of my head. We swayed in place as his rough hands took over the task of warming me, gently stroking my arms, my shoulders and back. My pulse pounded even harder in my ears, but gradually the cord of tension stiffening my spine eased although with everything that happened tonight and with Shane's arms now warm and solid around me, relaxed was more of a goal than an actuality.

Just when I was becoming deliciously aware that this grown man version of Shane was hard *everywhere*, he loosened his hold on me and stepped back. "Let's get those feet soaking in the tub." I may not have seen Shane in years but some things never changed. Right now he was tamping his tension with the same brusque, big brother bossiness I recalled from our childhoods. It took me a minute to feign nonchalance at what his proximity was doing to me and then I followed him down the hallway. "Hang on." He left me at the bathroom door and came back a minute later. "Here's something to change into." He handed me a neatly folded bundle—sweatpants and a tee shirt. "Go ahead." He angled his chin toward the bathroom behind me. "Take a shower if you want." I stepped backward into the bathroom with the clothing in my arms. He nodded and I took another step back till he pulled the bathroom door closed and then called through it. "I'll be out here. Shout if you need anything."

A shower was exactly what I wanted. If only I could scrub the entire nasty night away. Stepping out of my rented dress, sure that no drycleaner would ever get the scent of my panic-fueled sweat out of the fabric, I adjusted the temperature to the hottest I could stand, then pulled the pins out of my half up, half down hair. The shower was a blessing and a curse. I was desperate to erase the nasty residue of Rojas off me, his pain inducing hands, his overpowering cologne. But the cuts and bruises on the bottom of my feet came to stinging life under the hot spray. I'd feel like hell tomorrow because now with my adrenalin waning, my unaccustomed, barefoot, midnight run was making itself felt in every muscle. I wrapped myself in a towel, eager to get comfortable in sweats.

When I took a good look at the logo emblazoned on the black sweatpants I chuckled for the first time in days. Star Wars? Really? Flashing back to those long ago afternoons lounging on the Fortunatos' family room couch arguing over which Star Wars movie was the best ever, had me wondering how everyone else in the family was doing. They'd all be involved in careers by this time, even Shane's baby sister, Delaney. She'd only been twelve last time I saw her and oh man, did she hate the baby sister label. And then there was Christopher. Whatever profession he was pursuing, I'd no doubt he was acing it. I admit there were times in the last several years I forcibly pushed thoughts of Shane and his entire family to the back of my conscious mind. I didn't spend time on social media and I never sought out any of the

41

Fortunatos online. It was too painful to think about their lives moving forward when I was stuck wishing I was in the past with them.

My unconscious mind was another thing entirely. That's where my unquenchable thirst for Shane got free rein. Dreams of Shane was a steamy video I played on repeat most nights and those fantasies put my reality to shame. But now that I'm here with him I had to laugh. Wearing his extra-large, extra silly, Star Wars sweats and tee was so not the way I wanted him to see me after all this time. But yeah if Star Wars sweats meant I was here with flesh and blood Shane for a while who was I to argue with fate? I did a nosy check through his medicine cabinet, just to look for a comb and determined there was no female paraphernalia in his pristine bathroom. Either Shane didn't have a steady girlfriend or she wasn't the type who left all her stuff at his place. Finger combing my hair would have to do for now.

Shane's yard wide shoulders were hunched as he stared out the window, his thumb rhythmically scraping the label off the bottle of beer in his hand. He must've seen me in the window's reflection because he turned as I approached him and his half smile told me his thoughts were miles away. This Shane had more layers than the Shane of my childhood. His hooded eyes were impossible to read, his burnished five o'clock shadow was now in its eighth hour and his hair tufted out in fifty directions. But when he pulled another Fanta from the fridge and handed it to me, Shane morphed back to the boy of my childhood. The boy who looked out for me and everyone else. The boy I fell in love with.

Suddenly tongue-tied, I murmured. "The shower was just what I needed. Thanks."

He inclined his head and I plopped to sit cross legged in one corner of the nubby textured gray couch. We simply looked each other— every once in a while tipping our drinks for a swig. What was strange was, it wasn't strange. Being here with Shane, even after so many years, felt right.

That he was a cop now felt right somehow, too. If I have any memory of Shane, other than my fevered late night fantasies, it's of him looking out for his younger siblings. It came from being the eldest which he took seriously. He was the authoritative, young kid defender. Bossing them and bandaging them like he did with me tonight and dealing with bullies with a smart word or a quick fist was what he'd been doing from the first time I'd seen him.

"So." He tucked his chin into his chest. "Everything is set. There's an undercover squad patrolling the addresses you gave me, your place and where your dad is at."

"Thanks." I allowed my gaze to linger on the strong planes of his face, the set jaw, and world weary eyes. "It fits. You being a cop. You were always the ultimate big brother, the protector."

He grimaced into his beer then tipped the bottle up and gulped till it was done. After he walked it to the sink, he sat down again across from me, rubbing a hand over the scruff on his jaw. "No, Esme. Don't try to color me special. I wasn't there when it counted—when I was needed."

His response was not the self-deprecating joke I guess I'd expected, but something harsh and personal. "I don't understand." I tried to catch his gaze but Shane avoided mine, his big hands holding his splayed knees in a grip so tight his knuckles whitened.

"I was in the service. You and your family had moved away."

We'd stuck it out in the old neighborhood as long as we could. Mama loved our spacious one bedroom with a living area big enough for her piano and the sleeping alcove for me. My favorite part of our place was, hands down, our proximity to the Fortunatos. But we started having trouble paying the rent when the medical bills started piling up. After that first long hospital stay the summer Shane enlisted, we moved when the lease came up that fall. I only had a part-time job then. My parents insisted I finish at the Convent of the Sacred Heart rather than return to public school. I was only a year from graduating anyway. They also insisted I go straight to City College instead of working full-time but they didn't balk when I decided to spread my credits out over five years so I could fit more work hours around classes.

"Christopher got into Yale. My parents were over the moon about it. He even got a partial scholarship which was good because Ivy also got in."

"Wow. Both of them? That's amazing. For everybody." I missed the days when I knew all the news, all the ins and outs of the goings on in the Fortunato family.

"Yeah. You'd think so, right? But it wasn't. Not for long anyway." He bowed his head till his chin touched his chest. "Chris died of an overdose at the end of his first semester there."

"*Dios mio*, omigod, no! No. Oh, no. Shane, I can't believe… I'm so sorry. I didn't know." The tears I'd contained all evening streamed hot and fast down my cheeks but I ignored them, reaching for Shane, prying his hands off his knees and squeezing his fingers. He'd comforted me. I needed to return the favor. *Oh, Chris.*

"I was away when it happened. First year in the service. Some big brother." His raspy voice was deflated, defeated.

"C'mon. Did you have any clue something like that could happen?" I couldn't picture it. At all. Chris never did stuff like that. I would have known. We'd shared our deepest confidences. I'd confessed to Chris my feelings for Shane. He'd told me he was gay.

Shane rejected my theory with a quick shake of his head. "No one knows the details of it. Except there was a party. I

44

know Chris didn't do that shit but there's always a first time. In my gut I feel like it was probably the first time. We had a tough time getting accurate information. Point is, I take care of my sisters and brothers. But I wasn't there. Christopher needed me and I wasn't there." His words faded into a hoarse whisper as he slumped back against the couch.

"I don't think…"

"Trust me, Esme, you weren't there either. Believe me on this." The pain etched on his face made him look a decade older than his thirty-two years.

"I believe it was horrible, it's still horrible—for all of you. It will never stop being horrible. But it wasn't your fault." I believed that with my entire being. Just like Mama got cancer. Nobody's fault—just a terrible twist of fate.

"Yeah, so much time has passed and it hasn't gotten easier. We all…" He shook his head when no words emerged from his lips. If he hadn't just told me it happened years ago, I would've thought Shane was the vision of fresh grief. Because he blamed himself.

"I always loved your parents." I blushed as soon as the impulsive truth came out. Like I was making some sort of declaration. Was I so desperate to be part of the Fortunato family?

Shane's slow smile curved his wide lower lip and melted me like butter on hot toast. "And they always loved you, Esme. Losing Chris so close after you and your family left… my parents, my family—when they picked up their heads months later, no one had any idea where you'd moved."

"We moved to a cheaper apartment. And then another one. It was a…reactive time. Still is. We did what we could for Mama, to get by, including moving into the cheapest places we could find. Seems like we moved once a year. My father…changed. He was desperate to help Mama but nothing we did seemed to work…" My voice broke and I swiped at the tears still trickling down my face. I cried for Mama. For Christopher. Sweet, genius-smart Christopher who'd had a brilliant future ahead of him. Life was so unfair.

"Esme. Babe, don't cry. Please." He leaned forward to cup my chin, scraping his thumbs across my cheeks to brush away the tears that just wouldn't stop.

"I'm so sad about Chris."

"And I'm so sorry about your mom. But please...don't cry anymore." My head remained bowed as I sniffled, trying to stem the tide. His fingers nudged my chin up. "Hey, how about you come with me to Sunday dinner tomorrow?"

"You mean the big ones you always used to have with your family?" Oh man, the idea was so tempting. The Fortunatos used to invite me for dessert anytime one of them had a birthday. How cool would it be to see the rest of the family after all this time? *And spend more time with Shane*, the sneaky devil on my shoulder murmured.

"Yep. We still get together though not as often as the parents would like. They moved to Rockaway after...after."

Shane's appealing offer had the desired effect. My tears stopped and I lifted my chin. "I'd love to."

He grinned and the creases bracketing his cheeks widened and deepened. "Great. My parents will go nuts when they see you."

Just as I became hyper-aware of Shane's knuckle stroking soothing circles under my chin, just when I noticed the mesmerizing ring of gold surrounding the pupils of his sea blue eyes, and the tipsy sweetness of his ale warmed breath— just when my rapidly heating skin reminded me I was naked under the sweats and tee, Shane jerked back from me and stood. I followed suit, conscious of his fisted hands and stiff posture. Here we were, alone in the middle of the night at Shane's place. It was awkward and thrilling and pretty much my every imagining come true.

"Okay, little bird." In spite of the nickname it was a command. "It's late. You need sleep. Take the bedroom. My sheets are fresh—just changed them today. I'll bunk out here on the couch."

"No way, Shane. You take your own bed."

"Don't say another word. You know Ma trained us better than that. It's been a long day—for both of us. Look in the medicine cabinet, there's a spare toothbrush in there."

And that was Shane. Always the domineering big brother. Did he know the last thing I wanted to be was his little sister? Ugh, how embarrassing if he knew. But a couple of times tonight I'd battled a strong urge to show him I wasn't little Esme anymore but a full grown woman. Now I wished his sheets weren't laundered but smelled of him. And me. Together. We engaged in a little stare down as his set lips and determined eyes, concern creating faint fans of wrinkles at the corners, insisted I follow his direction. With a toss of my head I gave in. "This is only for your mom," I said with an exasperated twist of my lips.

Shane's bedroom was as organized and austere as my colorfully quilted single bed and jam-packed closet in our studio was messy. A spotless pale, gray rug took up most of the room and cushioned my injured feet as I shamelessly wandered around Shane's space absorbing every detail. The main detail was there were none. No personal items on display except a Mets ballcap hanging on the closet door-knob. Even the walls, painted a cloudy blue, held no art. I moved to a chest of drawers for a closer look at an eight by ten photo in a simple black frame that dominated the top of the tall oak dresser. Wow, the photo was taken the last time I'd seen Shane before tonight—the night of his going away party before the service. Mrs. Fortunato had corralled her kids in their big kitchen and oh yeah, now I remembered how Ivy pulled me into the group of siblings to stand next to her and her sisters. Shane and his brothers, all taller than the girls by that age, stood behind us, with Shane in the center. We all had our arms draped around each other and we were grinning like crazy. A weird kind of pit settled in my stomach when I saw myself in the photo. My teeth were showing in a huge smile but my eyes were solemn, like I knew that moment was a turning point. I'd seen Chris and the rest of the family here and there that summer but as the extent of Mama's illness became apparent, I felt guilty hanging out and having fun. If I wasn't at school or at my job, and I wasn't helping Mama then I was being selfish. When we moved I lost touch with everyone, remarkably simple to do as I was still without a cell phone back then. As the years passed I cherished the memory of my years living in the building next door to the Fortunatos, deeming them a crucial piece of an essentially happy childhood. I'd tried, over and over, to relegate my feelings for Shane into that same child-hood memories box, the honorary sibling box the family put me in against my will though it was better than nothing. But no matter what I did, or how I tried, Shane wouldn't stay put. His memory followed me into adulthood, causing me to measure every guy I encountered, usually a random colleague at work, against the sweet, fiercely protective boy I'd idolized since I was five.

I slid between the cool, white sheets on the king bed knowing full well I wouldn't sleep. Not with the events of tonight rampaging through my head. Not with the anger and sadness churning through me at Papá's deception and the news of Christopher's premature death. Not knowing Shane, all six foot two of warm, muscular sexiness, was only down the hall. Not knowing my father was still indebted to Reinaldo Rojas and I, his only form of payment, had run out on the sordid deal.

CHAPTER 6

SHANE

*H*ARSH STREAMS of light pulsed against my
eyelids forcing them open. I bolted to sitting
on the sofa, shoving the white throw, a soft, too small, girly
thing gifted me by my sister Holly, the Décor Queen, to the
floor.

Esme.

I clawed a hand through my hair as the entire evening
played back from the second I spotted her limping along
West Street till the moment I closed my bedroom door with
Esme under the quilt in my bed. My bed. There was no
scenario where I ever pictured Esme in my bed unless I was
there with her. But she was here, she was safe and I would
keep her that way.

I lowered the offending living room shades to half-mast,
then squinted at the digital readout on the microwave. Six
a.m. On auto-pilot I pressed the button on the machine for a
double espresso. After fishing ibuprofen out of the drawer
under the espresso machine I gulped it down with water and
carried the espresso to the shower.

Last night I'd downed a few too many beers as I contemplated this ugly situation and messaged my partner Alex as well as our supervisor to deliver the wild intel Reinaldo Rojas was in New York. What were the chances and looks like both our undercover squad and the Feds missed it. We already knew Rojas was careful. But now we could confirm his brass balls when he showed up in the city to host a well-attended party. Under federal indictment, but with money to burn, he excelled at keeping himself under the radar. For years we'd played his cat and mouse game, chasing down leads at the local level while the Feds mapped out the big picture tracking coke deliveries at our ports of entry and filing warrants. The ball was in our court now and it was past time to nab this guy.

Our supervisor would fill in the top brass and they'd have to involve the Feds who wanted him as bad as we did. This was our chance. With two federal warrants on him Rojas couldn't make a mistake. And because his tentacles were deep in this city we had to coordinate with our federal partners to make an arrest that would stick. Hard to believe but maybe this time we could finally nail the dope pushing bastard.

Toweling off, I checked my cell again. Lidia Goncalves, our supervisor, hadn't responded yet. I'd only given her vague info about the lead on Rojas, not that I knew much anyway, and I left Esme's name completely out of it. But Esme's name wouldn't remain out of it for long. I'd bet any money they'd want to use her to get to Rojas. Five minutes later I was dressed and Goncalves was on the line, telling me to sit tight till further instructions. When I reminded her today was my regular day off, she told me to go forth, enjoy but stay available via phone.

I scraped my damp hair back off my forehead, resisted the urge to drink cold OJ from the bottle and poured it into a glass. How was this even happening? How had Esme's father bartered his own daughter to pay a debt? My stomach twisted, souring the juice in my gut. When Esme told the story, shock set in and I had to disguise my revulsion. The man was her father but damned if I could ever forgive him. Last night the girl I knew, now the woman I pretty much figured I'd never see again but who I believed was happy and safe, narrowly escaped being given to and mauled by a notoriously ruthless drug kingpin. I was proud she outwitted Rojas's asshole guard and ran and grateful she was okay.

But underneath I was seething with twin needs—a gut deep desire to keep Esme safe even though God knows after last night she was firmly on Rojas's radar. As an undercover NYPD detective, I was an admittedly a local level cog in the Organized Crime Drug Enforcement Task Force. But I still burned to see Rojas in prison and hopefully spare who knows how many other families the pain of losing a loved one to overdose and addiction. Forcing my hands to uncurl from their fists, I pressed the button to make another coffee.

"Shane?" At her soft voiced query, blood raced straight from my brain to my manhood. No one else but Esme ever had the ability to do that to me. She consumed every part of me like she had from the first day we met. The only difference was now my body and thoughts, my wants and desires were those of a man. Esme was here with me now and the compulsion to keep her safe was stronger than the need to take my next breath.

She came down the hallway barefoot, looking rumpled and comfy, pretty much like my dream Esme. It was all I could do not to open my arms and gather her close. I cleared my throat. "I was getting another cup of espresso. What about you? What can I get you? English muffin okay?"

She stood beside me, and her essential scent was fresh and tantalizing even though the soap she used last night was mine and nothing if not basic.

"Whoa, sweet machine you have there, and yes, espresso and an English muffin sounds perfect."

I flashed back at Esme in our apartment back in the old days, standing politely at the door with hands folded till invited to sit while our rowdy family milled around the kitchen grabbing food and drinks like mini-barbarians.

"Coming right up." I loaded the toaster, dropped a pod into the machine, flipped the lever, then patted the appliance like a pet. "The family gave it to me the Christmas I moved in here. You know, cops and coffee. So..."

"Original," we finished at the same time. Esme grinned.

"You've gotta be hungry. I've got some eggs, I think. Maybe." I scratched the scruff on my chin. "How about juice?" My sisters and Finn consumed gigantic bowls of berries and protein packed smoothies most mornings but the contents of my fridge were as run of the mill plain as my undercover wardrobe of tee shirts and jeans.

"Whatever you're having is fine." She flipped her loose hair over her shoulder drawing my gaze to the bounce of her breasts. The tee shirt she wore was huge but my imagination filled in what the shapeless shirt left out.

"I usually save my appetite when my parents cook their Sunday dinners. You know how they go all out, especially when it's someone's birthday."

"I remember," she said. "A muffin and coffee are great. Hmm, let me think. Is it Finn's birthday?

"Look at you. Impressive memory. I can barely remember all of my siblings' birthdays." I buried my jealousy. Of course she remembered Finn's birthday. He was closer to her age, and she'd been witness to his teenage growth spurt, when his build, and the combo of his black hair and blue eyes mesmerized every girl in the neighborhood. His perfect looks embarrassed him back in the day but he'd soon learned to take advantage of nature's gifts. Shit, when she saw him now that he was always in training mode, now he was a buff, badass boxer, she wouldn't be any different than the entire population of the city who chased the lucky bastard.

"You don't fool me, Shane."

Her eyes crinkled at the corners as she held my gaze. Hard as I tried, I couldn't look away from those luminous eyes. I willed my cheeks not to redden as I raised my brows in query and watched her cup the espresso I proffered in her palm. As Ma always said, redheads, even my dull copper variety of the breed, wore their emotions for the world to see. Had Esme guessed? Did she figure out I was so into her, so enthralled with her memory these last ten years, that corrosive jealousy coated by stomach at the thought of her drooling over Finn?

"You're the best big brother. Of course you'd never forget a birthday. I'm only surprised..."

I dropped my gaze to my cup. I was jealous as fuck thinking about Esme and Finn but a nastier demon hovered, threatening to consume me. She knew I wasn't a good big brother. Christopher's death proved it. I squashed the thought. Every moment with Esme was a gift I never thought I'd get. I would not waste any moment with her dwelling on my shame.

"You're surprised about what...?"

Warm rose bloomed on her cheekbones. She shrugged. "I guess I'm surprised you're still single. Somehow I thought you'd be married with a bunch of kids by now..."

Her comment caught me by surprise and damn, I was so needy I basked in the idea she wondered about me at all over these last ten years.

"Yeah, well, you know, marriage should be forever and I..." I stumbled over my words as my neck heated, because yeah, my dream girl was standing right in front of me. "I... I'm still waiting for the right woman. But don't worry, my sisters are on my case, constantly pushing some unfortunate friend of theirs at me."

Esme pursed her lush lips. "Aw, poor Shane forced to date his sisters' friends. Sounds terrifying." Her bell like laugh rang out. "I seem to recall you always had a very healthy dating life. But if I'm really invited to Sunday dinner I need to get some clothes."

She glanced down at my funky cartoon sweats and again my gaze honed in on her breasts swelling against the tee shirt. God help me. This woman. This woman makes sweats sexy and I'm such a goner. Always have been. My mind wandered off on a sweet little journey then, where I pictured Esme in her clothes, then in my tee shirt and then in nothing at all. I jumped when the toaster dinged, yanked my gaze away from her luscious curves and quickly slathered butter over our muffins. I pushed a plate across the counter to her, then dropped my gaze to study the flecks of silver winking out of the quartz counter as I willed my body to stand down so I could focus on the issue at hand.

"Not at your place. You must know you can't go back there right now." The hair at the back of my neck stood at attention at the mere thought of Esme going anywhere near her place. Logic dictated if Rojas was pissed Esme got away and he had to be, he'd track her there. Calling her dad like she had to give him a heads up she ran on Rojas was more than the old man deserved, giving him ample time to evade Rojas. I resisted the urge to bring up her father again. Her father hadn't been so solicitous of Esme's wellbeing and safety last night. He'd sent her to meet Rojas blind, with no clue what she was walking in to. Esme realized she'd been done dirty by her dad even if she wouldn't say it out loud. But no way could she go anywhere near her apartment.

"I know." She mangled her bottom lip with her teeth.

"I still need a recent photo of your dad. Surveillance is organized and in position but a photo would help."

Her eyes widened and she dropped her half eaten muffin back onto her plate. "I forgot to tell you. The bodyguard took my cell last night. I can't believe I let him just take it..." She shook her head and even though she was looking at me I could tell her focus went inward. "That's why I borrowed your phone last night to call my father. I'm not on social media. Maybe I can access my email from your tablet? I think have a photo of him there."

My gut clenched as embarrassment, disgust, and revulsion raced across her face. In seconds, Esme morphed from the awkward of having breakfast with a childhood friend she hadn't seen in years to full recollection of her ordeal of last night. I couldn't stand to see the light sparking her vivid eyes go out. I didn't need to consult my supervisor or my team to know my next move. Esme would stay here, with me, while this played out. Rojas had her phone which meant he had her contacts. When she bailed last night he would've been furious. Ironic, but in this moment I acknowledged some small measure of reward for the pain I suffered at my lack of contact with Esme for so many years. There's no way Rojas would trace her here. I was best equipped to protect Esme by keeping her with me.

I grasped her elbow, led her to the couch and rested her plate on the coffee table in front of her. She sat in the corner opposite me, her bare feet tucked under her.

"Esme, don't go there. You got yourself out of a...nasty situation last night and I'm damn proud of you. Your father never should've put you in that position."

"I know. If he once treated me like an adult and clued me in, I could've thought of something. I could've come up with a solution. I guess we have to leave New York. At least that was my plan as of last night. Start over in Texas, change our names…"

"Rojas's operation has satellites everywhere. I don't know how long that plan would work. I'm undercover narcotics. You running into these…" I searched for a word suitable to her ears, "wrong dudes, is something I had to report. My supervisor and my partner now know Rojas is in the city. They'll involve our partners in the DEA and the DOJ." I shuttered my expression to conceal my disgust. Rojas had run rings around us for years and strolled into a hotel in midtown without our knowledge. "Let's take this step by step. For now, you don't go anywhere near your apartment."

"Right. Yes. I can't believe…" She didn't finish her sentence but she didn't have to. I bit back the tirade churning inside, my certainty that if her father cared anything about her he wouldn't have stuck her in such a vulnerable situation leaving her completely in the dark about the kind of garbage Rojas was. If he cared at all, he wouldn't have set up the meeting with Rojas in the first place. Hadn't Esme said Rojas knew she was a virgin? Holy fuck, that information alone was enough to make my blood boil. My scorn for Esme's father was morphing into something dangerous. Esme was too kind-hearted, too forgiving for her own good. I swallowed back the bile threatening to choke me and schooled my voice to polite policeman.

"The surveillance team will watch out for your father. See if you can find a recent photo of him. You've done what you should do. You spoke to him so he knows you're okay." Which was way more than he deserved. I left the thought unsaid. I forced a comforting smile and kept it in place till her lips curved up, a weak version of her usual megawatt smile but something. "Now let's figure out something for you to wear today."

Esme raised her brows and shot out a quick, "no way,"

when I presented her with a pair of my gym socks before we took the elevator down to the underground garage. "I look ridiculous enough in your sweats, Shane."

I raised mine in response as we engaged in short battle of wills. Ridiculous was not the descriptor I would go for. In my sweats Esme's body should've looked lumpy but though the clothing covered her well enough, she still managed to look like a goddess. "You need to protect your feet." I found an extra pair of flips flops, size huge in my trunk and she took off the socks to put them on. Thank fuck, because she would've worn the socks or I would've carried her around till we bought her shoes. We ended up driving to a Target near my parents' home in Rockaway. Once inside the store, Esme bee-lined for the spring dresses, stopping in front of a coral one to run a finger along the neckline. We looked at each other and she pressed her lips together.

"I can't afford to buy stuff I don't need." She was pissed, her jaw set at a stubborn angle.

"No choice. My squad will foot the bill."

"No, they will not. I can buy my own clothes since I have to. And the sooner I get out of your sweats, the better." Her innocent statement hit me straight in my manhood and reignited a full-on fantasy where we skipped the family dinner to satisfy more private appetites. And it stood to reason if I thought Esme looked luscious and adorable wearing my clothes, every other guy in this Target did too. My gaze performed a slow reconnaissance of our immediate vicinity. All I saw were women of various ages running hands along racks of dresses like Esme was.

"I better forget about wearing a dress because anyone seeing my scraped knees will have questions." I nodded and willed my hardening body to relax as I marched double time to keep up with her as she strode over to where women's casual clothing was displayed, saying over her shoulder. "I have to admit, I'm a little weirded out seeing your family again after so long. After we do this, I'll want to go somewhere to buy flowers."

"Sure." I caught up to her and couldn't resist. I ran my thumb along the faint line between her eyebrows soothing away the anxious frown and relishing the softness of her skin. "Okay, flowers, sure. No call to be nervous though. When I texted Mom you were coming, she was thrilled. It'll be fun, just like back when we were kids."

CHAPTER 7

*D*ID Shane know what he did to me with his offhand comment about *back when we were kids?* Meeting him again, even the unusual way we had, was something I'd dreamed about since I was fifteen. Only the knowledge Shane was outside the door allowed me to finally relax into sleep last night. Did he have to keep talking about the old days? Would he always see me as the little kid next door? I was one hundred percent not a kid anymore.

Pressing my lips together in a way my mom always said gave away my stubborn nature, I shimmied out of Shane's sweats and tee shirt in the Target restroom. I paid for the purchases, again refusing Shane's offer to do so and removed the tags. These basics weren't dressy enough to attend my first dinner with the Fortunatos in ten years but there was no way I was going to wear a dress and have to explain the state of my messed up knees and feet to Shane's family.

Shane's offhand remark about a Sunday dinner being a throwback to our childhoods sparked something dangerous inside me. I decided to test how Shane actually saw me these days and the results were eye opening. He wasn't as immune to me as he seemed. At least I didn't think so. With no brothers and zero experience of the opposite sex aside from some coffee dates with a work colleague or two, I was guessing. Even college had been devoid of opportunities to date, my work schedule and my mother's needs kept me running from one thing to the next—with little time to hang out with girlfriends, never mind foster a relationship with a guy. And I wasn't into hookups. For one thing I lived at home with my parents, now only my father. For another, I was an introvert. Some of my girlfriends were on dating apps and I'd started setting myself up on a couple of sites, a half a dozen times, only to chicken out at the last minute.

Outerwear choices in hand, I kept browsing. Shane was in protective mode, dogging my steps. I had to know. Did Shane still see me as a kid? If he did, would that always be the way he viewed me? I stopped in front of a display of bras and thongs. Last night I'd arrived at Shane's apartment with just the clothes on my back. In the shower, I'd rinsed out the underthings I'd worn yesterday. Just now Shane nodded in casual approval at my selections as I chose jeans, a tee shirt, a flowy blouse and flats.

I selected a few lacey thongs in neon summer shades and lifted them on their tiny hangers, turning to Shane. I tilted my head in inquiry. "I like these. What do you think?" The same question I'd asked him about the other clothes I'd chosen. How would he react now? Like I was a kid?

Twin coins of color ruddied Shane's cheekbones. His eyes widened and his Adam's apple bobbed in his throat. "Fine," he bit out gruffly. "They're... fine," he said again. He turned away, effectively blocking me from the gazes of the other shoppers with his massive back but I summoned him again with a tap on his shoulder.

"Okay, thanks. Can you hold these for a sec?" Without waiting for a response, I plopped the clothing into his waiting arms, the thongs sitting right on top. His jaw hardened as he examined the undies. He nodded twice before a grunted "yeah" emerged. The clothing rested across his corded arms like he was a robo-valet. Deciding not to test him further, I grabbed a white bra in the same lacey pattern, threw it over the others and led the way to the cash register.

When I came out of the rest room in my new clothing, Shane was standing right outside the door, arms folded across his chest, a forbidding expression on his face. I executed a small pirouette and finished it with hands on my hips. He nodded once as his lips mashed together. "Good. Great," he said through his teeth. "C'mon. You said you wanted to get flowers?"

I nodded back, hiding a grin. *Go, me*. Shane did *not* consider me a kid anymore.

We pulled up at a flower shop on Rockaway's main boulevard. The beachy Queens neighborhood was definitely part of the city and yet this section oozed a relaxed surfer vibe. Once I stepped inside the shop, I was nearly floored by the overpowering scent of cut blooms. The multiple vases of cut lilies and lily plants which were so popular around Easter time, transported me back to my mother's wake and funeral. The abundant blooms were one more thing we gave her which we couldn't afford. I heaved in a strangled breath feeling like I was suffocating and knew I'd never willingly go near lilies again. Head aching, light headed, I turned to see Shane with his arms folded across his chest chatting with the man behind the register.

"That looks good." I said faintly, pointing to a full, glossy leafed fern. Shane carried it out while I paid for it. Once I was back in the Jeep, I grabbed my water bottle from the cupholder and took a long drink.

"You okay, Esme?" Shane's all-seeing gaze studied my face.

"Thirsty," I said, wishing for my sunglasses. The sun was high and bright in the noon sky and Shane's observant cop eyes missed nothing. "The flowers...the scent...I didn't realize they would hit me so...yuck, I think I'm gonna throw up."

"Okay, I've got you. Slow, deep breaths, Esme. Really slow. That's it. The weirdest things bring you back, right? Go ahead put your head between your knees, if you want. I'm right here. I'm not going anywhere." His hand came out to rub my back and the warm weight of it, the solid strength of it, was what I'd been missing. I seldom displayed my grief to my father. He'd been, still was, so broken up about Mama's death, I tended to comfort him first and deal with my own pain later—in private. Or not at all. I sucked in deep breaths counting them slowly till my stomach righted itself. When I picked up my head, Shane was staring at my profile. He put a forefinger under my chin, turning my face to his. A deep line creased the skin between his thick eyebrows, as he examined my face, not allowing me to look away till he finished his thorough scrutiny.

"I'm okay now." I forced a smile and magically his worry line disappeared as he nodded.

"It comes in waves, right?" His nod reassured me my weird lightheaded moment was perfectly normal. "I know. I'm here for you, Esme. You don't have to hide your feelings with me." How had he guessed that was exactly what I'd been doing all these months?

He lowered the Ray Bans back onto his nose, and shifted the Jeep into gear. I loved every economical movement of his broad hands. Shane, the study in contrasts. Gentle voice soothing me out of a sick stomach and protective cop focused on his dangerous job. Both essential Shane traits and I was beginning to wonder how I'd ever gotten along without him for ten years and how I'd survive when we parted.

When I woke up this morning for a few seconds I thought I'd imagined last night's events. Everything about Rojas was the stuff of nightmares and Shane's appearance pure wish fulfillment. I thanked every deity who'd granted my wish to see Shane again and I couldn't help but think I needed to come clean, tell him my feelings for him were far from sisterly even if it meant he'd reject me. For ten years I'd wondered what Shane was doing, agonized over who he might be with, fantasized about the two of us and kicked myself for not telling him how I felt when I had the chance. Fifteen-year-old Esme had been blindsided by her feelings for Shane and devastated by her mother's illness. Twenty-five-year-old Esme owed it to herself to close the loop of her relationship with Shane once and for all.

Shane mostly kept to the speed limit, giving me and my queasy stomach a chance to settle, and ten minutes later we pulled up to a rambling, stone and clapboard, two story house. The cheery teal door and amply cushioned rocking chairs welcomed. We snagged the last spot at the front of the driveway and ever the big brother, Shane muttered about Delaney and Leo's clunkers jammed haphazardly behind his parents' SUV.

"What a beautiful house. So your parents moved here when...?"

"Yeah. After Christopher...being in the city, our apartment...it was too hard on them. On all of us. They needed a change of atmosphere and since they both have cousins in the area, this works for them. Delaney and Leo are the only ones still at home though. I only lived here for a short time after I got discharged. Ivy and Holly live in Manhattan now, and Finn has a place in Brooklyn. It's rare we're all together these days."

I swallowed hard but I could still hear my heart beat pounding in my ears as I trailed behind Shane up the short flight of brick steps. We'd barely stepped onto the small porch when the front door was swung wide and I was enfolded into the giant embrace of none other than the family patriarch. Joseph Fortunato was a bear of a man as befit his occupation as a mover. He'd owned his company as long as I had known the family. From what Shane said, each of the siblings worked at the company at some point with Leo and Delaney still employed in the family business.

"Esme! Willya look at you, all grown up and pretty as a picture. It's been a while, eh?" His jovial, soothing voice was as comforting as the rumble of a freight train into a distant station and went a long way toward quelling my fear of seeing the family after so long. I grinned big into his shoulder, absurdly grateful to see him again.

"It's been a long time, Mr. Fortunato. But I'm so happy to be here."

He frowned at my formality and touched my chin with a gentle, thick forefinger. "Esme, it's Joe or if you want, Pop," he said, before moving past me and settling his pawlike hands on Shane's shoulders. "Good to see you, son."

"Same here, Pop," Shane answered. His brief words were heartfelt and full of respect.

"C'mon, now, your mother is cookin' up a feast and everyone's here already…I mean not…oh you know what I mean." One look at his face with his chocolate eyes glistening and I knew Mr. Fortunato—Joe, was referring to Christopher. I totally got how the sadness just crept up, the unexpected tears when a thought went sideways and a memory popped up. How much harder it had to be for the Fortunatos to cope with Christopher's sudden death? At least Papá and I had some time to mentally prepare.

The foyer was cozy with the same shabby-chic, half-moon hall table I remembered from years ago holding the same yellow ceramic bowl overflowing with a jumble of keys. Yet even with that familiar sight, I still froze at the sound of the voices and laughter coming from a room down the short hall to the right. Once again, I was the shy only child come to visit but I knew what would make me feel better.

"Where's the kitchen?" I tugged the plant from Shane's hands. He gave me a long look but said nothing, angling his head left.

I poked my head into the well-lit, efficiently laid out room with an abundance of white painted cabinets dominated by a massive commercial stove and spotted Shane's Mom exactly where I knew she'd be. Clare had hardly changed at all. She might have a few more freckles and the very faintest lines fanning out from the corners of her eyes but only a touch of silver threaded through her now chin-length, dark auburn hair.

Clare and Joe had always shared the cooking duties for their family but after a long day as the bookkeeper for the family business Clare always said cooking was her creative outlet. She stood stove-side as if conducting an orchestra, button-down white shirt and jeans under an apron and ballet flats on her feet, pouring fresh peas and sliced mushrooms into a large sauté pan where sizzling garlic and olive oil already scented the room. Breaded chicken tenders browned on another burner. She expertly lifted the cutlets onto a strategically stationed, paper towel covered platter, before transferring her focus back to the mushrooms and peas and adding a cup of broth. As I inhaled the heady fragrance combinations, I realized I'd consumed nothing since breakfast yesterday until the English muffin at Shane's place a few hours ago.

"Hi Mrs. um, Clare. It's me. Esme."

She turned at the sound of my voice. Her eyes, the same stormy blue as Shane's, crinkled as she gifted me a warm, welcoming smile. Leaving the wooden spoon in its rest she opened her arms. I deposited the plant on the butcher block island and ran into them. I was crying and I couldn't help it. But it was okay because she was crying too.

"Oh, sweet girl," she crooned. "It's so good to see you again. I'm so sorry about your poor mother. There now, let me get a proper look at you." She stepped back from me, taking in my new white jeans and Easter egg lavender tee. She clucked her tongue. "Lovely as ever," she said in a voice which I guess would always carry a faint lilt of Ireland. She ran soft, gentle fingers over my cheeks and hair before she folded me into her arms again and it felt like heaven to be in her embrace. I missed my mother. For the last couple of years she'd been too sick to hug me like I wanted her to and I'd been terrified of hugging her too hard and possibly hurting her. "I'm so sorry…about Chris." I whispered into her honey and lemon scented neck.

"Oh, I know. I know. Such a loss. Such a terrible, unfathomable loss. Some days I still can't believe it, you know? There now, Esme. Hush, it's alright, sweet. Let me see that big smile of yours."

For some reason the tears streamed unabated down my cheeks even though I was smiling now. We stepped back from each other again, but continued to embrace at the elbow, me reluctant to let go. Then Clare reached for a tissue from the box behind her, handed me one and took another for herself.

"I'd say we both feel the better now for having a good cry, isn't that right?" Clare caught my gaze and tilted her head in question.

I nodded back with a slightly less watery smile, not trusting my voice. She wiped her eyes efficiently and tucked the tissue inside her apron pocket. "Sometimes it's what a body needs."

"Yeah, but I bet my eyes are red." Right now I regretted my decision not to spend money on makeup at Target. Here I was seeing the Fortunatos for the first time in ten years and my eyes were swollen and red. Several deep breaths later, I shook back my hair and swiped a knuckle under each eye as I regained my composure. I'd no idea I'd react this way seeing Shane's mom again but I shouldn't have been surprised. She'd always been so accepting of me, the kid from next door hanging around with her brood. She was as warm as the biscuits I could smell baking in the oven. I couldn't stay away then and I couldn't now.

"Here, let me." She eased the tissue out of my tight grip and dabbed it under my eyes. "You look as beautiful as ever with your big beautiful eyes and those naturally sooty lashes. I'm glad you're here, Esme. We've missed you. Especially Shane."

I startled at her words, heat flooding my cheeks. What did she mean *Shane* missed me? "Shane?" I choked out his name.

"I've got eyes in my head, Esme. Anyone could see the bond between you two, even when you were kids." She looked me in the eye, daring me to counter her statement.

"But we haven't seen each other in ten years."

"And yet...here you are." She continued to hold my gaze even as I lifted my chin, fighting the uncomfortable sensation of having my every secret laid out for scrutiny like the vegetables spread out on her butcher block table.

What could I say? It was complete serendipity Shane and I had met up last night after so long. Clare adjusted the gas to simmer on the mushroom pan, turned off the heat under the chicken, checked under the lid on a pan of rice sitting on a back burner before pulling the biscuits out of the oven and setting them on the butcher block and covering them with a tea towel. "This'll all keep for a sec. I can't keep ya to myself in here. Come out and say hello to everyone."

Clare took my wing as I left the kitchen and entered the living area. Everyone was rising from the enormous sectional flanking the coffee table to stream out to the dining room visible through an arched opening.

"Es-mer-al-da!" That was Ivy. Her long, pin straight blonde hair flew back from her shoulders as she ran to me. Lithe in her flowy flowerchild dress, she looked about seventeen although I knew her to be twenty-six. She was the closest to me in age and Christopher's twin.

I enclosed her in a long hug. "Ivy, I'm so sorry," I whispered in her ear.

"I know, I know, thank you," she whispered back.

Leo's voice boomed then, his deep baritone much the same as Joe's which was weird since he was the adopted Fortunato child. "How 'bout we bring this cheery tribe to the table?" He stepped behind me then spun me around to plant a quick kiss on my cheek. "Welcome home, Esme." I could feel my eyes start to fill again as I stood on tip toe to return the peck to his cheek. "Thanks, Leo."

I was overrun then by Delaney, Holly and Finn who swarmed into a circle to hug me and issue words of welcome. Throughout, Shane stood on the sidelines, his smile wide and reassuring as I was embraced by the exuberant Fortunato clan. We all migrated to the dinner table, everyone finding their usual seats leaving me to the right of Shane who was at the head of his end of the long polished pine table they'd always had. Ivy was at my other side. Joe, with Clare at his right, presided at the opposite end facing Shane.

I swallowed, still consumed with shyness, but I had no cause for worry. Conversation lapsed while we all indulged. There was laughter and food and more food until it was time for coffee and cake. After perfect biscuits, breaded chicken cutlet, mushroom and pea risotto, and a giant green salad, I was patting my stuffed belly along with the rest of the family.

"Gather round now." That was Joe. "Let's all sing 'Happy Birthday' to Finn." Clare pushed open the kitchen door, a giant homemade chocolate frosted sheet cake with candles shaped two and nine already lit. All eyes shifted to Finn as we sang. With his short, wavy ebony hair, blue eyes and muscled physique, Finn was, hands down, one of the most handsome men I'd ever seen and that included guys in movies, sports, television—anywhere.

All of the Fortunatos were good looking, even great looking, in their own way. I, of course, would always believe no one compared to Shane with his laughing eyes and eldest brother protective personality. He was my first friend in a new country when I'd had none. No matter what happened or didn't happen between us, I'd never forget him. If I hadn't been able to push him out of my mind these past ten years it only proved I never would. Christopher and his twin Ivy were lissome in looks, Chris had been a slim, tall, classically handsome blond who usually went for a goth look with black boots and a silver earring. Leo, not a Fortunato by birth, took after his leonine name with a head of wild, golden-brown hair, full beard and a physique to match. And *Dios*, the Fortunato women were all gorgeous in their own right. Holly, Ivy, and Delaney were each a different striking combination of their parents' Italo-Irish ancestry.

But Finn? He was next level handsome. The promise of his deep set, soulful blue eyes and the classic features I'd recalled from ten years ago had been born out in the now twenty-nine year old athlete with chiseled features and a flawlessly proportioned body. His nose wasn't the perfect blade I recalled though. It'd been broken. When we finished singing, he raised a broad hand to push back the falling spikes of his hair then his heavy lashed, hooded gaze focused as he blew out the candles on his cake. When he looked up moments later, he swiped a hand again at his hair and I realized it was a nervous tic. Faint color appeared on his sculpted cheekbones as he said, "th-thanks, everybody."

Everyone burst into applause and additional happy birthdays and I joined in. Finn had always been a person of few words. As a kid, and as a shy foreigner, I'd probably never said more than hello to him whenever we met. It took me a while to figure out he had a stutter and that bullies taunted him in a grade school. Shane and Leo were his steadfast defenders from the beginning but they couldn't be everywhere and as Finn grew older and bigger, he learned to use his fists to combat his tormenters. From what I'd gathered today, Finn continued to develop those skills and lately carved a place for himself on the regional boxing circuit, much to Clare Fortunato's dismay. From what his family said, Fighting Finn Fortunato was racking up wins in the light heavyweight division. It saddened me to see even in the midst of family, Finn seemed uncomfortable as a speaker. Not that any of his siblings noted the stutter by word or deed. But all eyes were on him for his birthday and even though they were loving eyes, the scrutiny was clearly difficult.

"Okay, okay, time to open your gift, Finn." Delaney, at twenty-two the youngest Fortunato, was all but levitating in her chair with excitement. "Always in a r-r-rush, eh, Laney?" Finn stretched his arm and used his massive palm to mess up the top of Delaney's bright copper hair.

She squirmed out of his reach. "Not in too much of a rush. I finished my cake. But we voted on this." Her cornflower eyes shone with anticipation. "We think you're gonna love it."

"Oh yeah? B-Bet I will too." Finn made short work of tearing off the striped blue paper covering the big box.

"Oh, wow this c-cool. I definitely wanted one of these n-ninja smoothie machines." He pushed back his short hair again. "Looks complicated though. Maybe need a c-college degree to work it." He flashed his bright white teeth at his self-deprecating joke. But Clare Fortunato chose not to see the humor.

Clare set down the thermal pitcher she was using to pour coffee into mugs and planted her hands flat on the table in front of her. "There's nothin' wrong with yer brain, Mr. Muscles. I'd be a lot happier if you'd go back to school and quit getting yer head bashed in." Her brogue still thickened when she got emotional, same as when we were kids. She folded her arms across her chest.

Joe reached up to stroke his palm over her elbow. "This isn't the time, Clare. It's the boy's birthday."

Clare's lips compressed as she resumed pouring coffee and I saw the sheen of tears in her vivid eyes. Finn bolted to his feet and raised both hands scraping them through his hair. "Not everybody goes to c-college, Ma. We're not all smart like…"

Ivy sprang up then too, her slim frame vibrating with emotion. She leaned across the table to address her mother and brother. "Enough. Not another word from anybody. This is your birthday celebration, Finn. For what it's worth I agree with Mom. But listen everybody, Finn is an adult and capable of making his own choices. I love you no matter what, Finn. And anyway, we have a guest."

Everyone's gazes swiveled to me and scalding heat climbed from my chest to my hairline. What to say? The Fortunatos weren't my family even if I'd spent my youth wishing they were. I had no business weighing in on their lives.

"Aw, Esme's more like a sister than a guest," Leo said. And there it was. I was the honorary sister.

"I've missed you all. Thanks for inviting me and for the

hospitality you've always shown me." Everyone relaxed back into their seats, taking mercy on me.

Ivy was handing coffee mugs around as Clare continued to pour it. She offered a mug to me. "Cream and sugar, Esme?"

I opened my mouth to answer but before I could respond, Shane jumped in. "Esme doesn't take cream. Lactose intolerant." He made the off the cuff assertion—accurately, without looking up from his plate as he lifted a forkful of birthday cake to his mouth. He didn't see the eyebrow-raise on every single member of his family but I did and heat scalded my cheeks. Were they all thinking Shane and I were hooking up? If only. Or...

"Oh, yeah, riiiight. I forgot," Ivy said. "What a phenomenal memory you have, Shane." Her sisterly sarcasm was on full display and I was only a bystander caught in the crossfire. Shane raised his gaze from his cake to encounter the avid stares of his entire family. Red flags flashed across his cheekbones but Shane wasn't the eldest for nothing. He owned it, winking at me, ignored them all and took another big forkful of cake.

"You know what my father always said?" Joe asked the table at large, jumping in to soothe the fray.

"I remember, Pop," Leo said. "Your dad had a lot of sayings but I think the one you're remembering now is: *if you are more fortunate than others, it is better to build a longer table than a taller fence.*"

"Exactly. You're welcome back to our table any time, Esme. I hope we see a lot more of you in the future. Just how did you and Shane reconnect anyway?" His deceptively genial dark eyes zeroed in on me shrewdly and Shane and I both looked at each other. Neither of us wanted to lie. A generalized truth was better than an outright lie. "We kind of ran into each other on West Street the other day," I said.

Joe nodded, his gaze still skimming over me thoughtfully.

"Fate, then," Clare Fortunato declared with a firm nod. The back of Shane's neck turned brick red but he said nothing, only took his time scooping up the last chunks of his cake.

"Not like you to be at a loss for words, Shane." Holly piped up with a speculative glance at her brother. Actually, Holly had been rather subdued today as well. Not at all like the Holly I remembered who was usually overflowing with opinions and not afraid to share them.

"Not like you either," Shane said, verbalizing my thought.

"Work stress," Holly said with a decisive jerk of her chin, the kind Clare always issued which, translated meant, *that's all I'm gonna to say— so quit asking.*

"Same," said Shane, as he graced his sister with a brotherly smirk.

"Are you a cop too, Holly?" I asked. There were a couple of choked guffaws. Okay. The answer was negative. My face heated again even as my chin lifted a fraction. "I haven't seen any of you in years so give me a break, okay? Just wondering what the work stress was?"

"Only teasing, Esme. Sorry." That was Leo. "But Holly—a cop?" He lifted his shoulders and dropped them as he gazed pointedly at Holly's perfect, chin length raven hair and the fresh silk blouse that worked effortlessly with her French jeans.

"Quit while you're ahead, my brother. There's plenty of capable, female, well-dressed, cops out there. We women do it all and we do it in high heels, am I right, Esme? Shane?" Holly nudged Shane then turned to me. "I started my own business. Dad gave me the green light to expand my home staging business beyond the moving company into a full-fledged interior design company. "So I took the leap. It's exciting but I'm crazy busy and a little overwhelmed."

Holly had always possessed the most sophisticated fashion instinct of any teenager I knew even counting the girls who went to the Convent of the Sacred Heart with me and had cash to burn on clothing. Made sense she now employed her unique style for a home design business.

"Wow, congratulations, Holly. That's fantastic. It must be exhausting starting your own business." As I sat back in my seat I didn't miss the way Delaney chewed the corner of her lip and looked over at her mother rather than Holly. Seeing this family after so much time was strange. Everyone was now an adult, even Delaney, with a life of his or her own. It was tough pulling all the threads together.

"Esme, what do you do for work? Are you seeing anyone special?" Holly changed the subject back to me and I have to admit I was caught off guard because in the old days there was usually so much going on with the Fortunatos I never had to pop out of my shell too much. But now I had to disclose the fact of my non-existent love life to the entire Fortunato family.

"I'm in medical research for blood cancers at Sloan Kettering." I lifted a shoulder. "With long hours and...everything, I don't have a lot of time to date."

"I'm thinking of going on some dating apps," Delaney piped up. "My friends say it's hit or miss but you never know."

I grinned at Delaney. "I've been looking into them too."

"Apps now, is it? Doesn't anybody meet the old-fashioned way anymore, you know face to face?" Clare, as ever not shy with her opinion, weighed in.

"Oh Mom, it's just one more way to meet someone, not the only way. Because you never know, right Esme?" Delaney grinned oh man the impish Delaney I remembered was back, always trying to catch up to what her older siblings were doing.

I looked around the table at this beautiful family. As far as I knew the Fortunato sibs had always had active social lives but I hadn't seen any of them in ten years and no one mentioned anyone special today. Wouldn't significant others have been invited to Finn's birthday lunch? Maybe not. I'd been invited solely because I was a recently reconnected honorary sibling, wasn't I? Socializing with significant others was no doubt reserved for the proper setting— maybe they were all looking forward to seeing someone this very evening. I shook off the feeling that maybe if I'd met Shane for the first time now instead of twenty years ago, I wouldn't have the honorary little sister label attached to me. That's when I remembered my promise. I never thought I'd reconnect with Shane. But I had and I would at least let him know how I felt. If he still couldn't view me any other way than as a kid, at least I would know that once and for all.

"Right," I replied. "What's that old commercial? You gotta be in it to win it?"

"That's for the lottery," Shane corrected, totally not getting the joke. Then he scraped his chair back so fast it almost toppled over. He righted it, saying, "I know we all have work tomorrow." I rose too, happy to put an end to the quiz about my seriously lacking love life.

"Thanks so much, everyone, it was wonderful to see you all again," I said. "I'm glad I got to share in Finn's birthday celebration. Happy birthday again, Finn."

Finn inclined his head and smiled his charismatic smile. Multiple hugs and kisses later, Shane's hand was hot on my back as we made our way to the front door. When we got there Ivy was trailing us. "Esme, hang on. Not so fast. I don't want to lose touch again. We need get together…it's been way too long. Let's do coffee sometime."

"I'd love to." I hugged Ivy tight as Shane stood silent at my side his impatience telegraphed from his exaggerated breaths.

"I'm a grad student now and I work part-time. I have a studio near Colombia," Ivy said. "I'll give you my number. You do have a phone these days, I hope?" We both laughed.

"I do. But I actually don't have it on me right now. I work uptown too— on the east side though so maybe we can meet in the middle somewhere?"

"Sure. Shane can give you my number." Ivy stepped back fast as Shane hustled me out giving her brother a side-eye which he returned with a vengeance.

CHAPTER 8

SHANE

I'D OPENED the passenger door for Esme when Mom came rushing down the steps with a reusable grocery bag. She held it up. "You forgot your leftovers," she called. Mom's voice could go from soft to piercing in a nano-second. Right now her words probably reached our second cousins out in Brooklyn.

"Hang on." Esme hurried back to meet her at the bottom step. Impatient to be gone, ready to have some alone time with Esme, I watched as Ma handed over the bag, pulled Esme into a one armed hug and whispered something in Esme's ear. Esme said something back, returned the hug and stood waving as Mom climbed the steps and went back into the house.

I took the bag and set it on the floor of the back seat while Esme settled into the passenger. Once I was in my own seat I examined Esme's profile. "You and Ma were thick as thieves back there," I said. "Talking about me?"

Thanks to me blurting out my recollection of her milk allergy, my entire family was now clued in regarding my undying attraction to Esme. And while I didn't care they knew, it would suck when they felt sorry for me if Esme moved on with her own life without me after we dealt with Rojas. Would she move on? My sisters, no slouches when it came to family inquisitions, got her to admit she wasn't dating anyone. But there was no doubt if she wanted a guy—the guy would want her back. She was Esme. If she didn't work so much and if she didn't have this looming crisis with Rojas to deal with, she could have anybody she wanted. Like Lori made clear: not every woman wants a guy who carries a weapon. And Esme deserved the best. A guy who was highly educated. Refined. Someone who wore a suit to work and belonged to a country club.

But I wasn't gonna give up without a fight. Not after we found each other after so much time. I shook myself out of my mood. I had my dream girl right next to me—right now. If she gave me any inkling that she returned my feelings...

Esme examined my profile and her lips took on a teasing curve. "You're funny, Shane. Do you think your mom and I can't have a conversation without it being all about you?"

"That's exactly what I think." I chuckled at the disbelieving way she shook her head.

"Someone is so full of himself." she said. The scornful twist of her lips was still there but when she evaded my direct gaze, I was certain *I* was their topic of conversation.

"What can I say? I know my mother." I threw out the bait.

"Oh yeah? I guarantee you'll never guess what she said." Boom. She went for it.

"Then I guess you'll have to tell me."

"No way." She made a zipping motion with her fingers across her delectable lips.

"Then I guess I have no choice. I'll have to tickle you." I shrugged again like there was nothing I could do about it.

She sucked in an outraged gasp. "You wouldn't *dare*. You know how ticklish I am!"

"I do recall something like that," I said. Of course I remembered. I remembered everything. When my hand was halfway to her taut stomach I paused and used my Darth Vader voice. "One——last—chance, Esme. *Tell me.*"

She shook her head vehemently, eyes wide with excited anticipation. My hand descended to her ribs and in seconds I had her doubled over. Her eyes streamed and her laughter filled the car, buoyant as balloons.

After one last swipe over the unbelievably soft skin of her hip, I reluctantly slid my hand out from under the hem of her tee shirt because damn, I was enjoying this game way too much. It was past time to cool the hell off. "Give?"

"Yes! Okay." Her words emerged on a sultry, ultra-feminine laugh. I caught her gaze. "So?" I said. After a bunch of soft exhales she said, "Okay. I'll tell you but you won't like it."

"Try me." Our little game had fogged up the windows and I was acutely aware Esme was not the ten year-old who was tickle-teased back in the day by us Fortunato kids till we were told in no uncertain terms by our mother to lay off.

"Your mom said…" She twisted completely in her seat to face me and waited till I turned toward her as well. "She said when Shane gives his heart, he gives it forever and that…I'd never find a fiercer protector than you."

Whoa. This was not what I expected when I saw Ma and Esme talking. I thought Mom told Esme a joke or an embarrassing story about me. Damn. Under Esme's scrutiny the back of my neck burned. Much as I tried I couldn't relax my clenched fists and bunched shoulders. Fact was, Mom was one hundred percent right. Did Esme know she'd captured my heart that first summer almost twenty years ago?

"You said something to Mom too." I held her gaze.

"I did." Her voice was light but her eyes darkened to a solemn forest green.

"Care to share it?" I raised a brow and forced a neutral tone again even though my heart was galloping out of my chest.

She tilted her chin up, as she continued to meet my gaze. "I told her....my heart was given a long time ago. I'd already found my only one."

God, what was she saying? What did that cryptic statement signify? *Esme. Tell me.* My voice sounded hoarse to my ears. I cupped her jaw, not allowing her to turn away. "Please."

"You, Shane. It's always been you. You're my only one." Every one of her whispered words hit me like the answer to a prayer.

"I'm gonna kiss you now." It wasn't a request.

"Feels like I've been waiting forever for you to do that." Her lush lips curved up again. Her smile was endearingly shy and somehow, at the same time, everything provocative.

I stroked a thumb along her jaw. "I could never kiss you before. But God how I wanted to. I couldn't let myself. But now..."

"Shane," she responded raising her dark brows. "Are you going to keep *talking* about it?

Her sly smile wound me up tight. One swift movement and my hand was at the small of her back. Another second and I'd pulled her in so fast, her warm breath puffed out. I ran my tongue along the seam of her lips, tasting her. Our first real kiss, and it was perfect. Better than any dream. I'd fantasized about kissing Esme for so long I couldn't remember a time I hadn't wanted this one thing more than anything else I'd ever desired—including being a cop.

It took more control than I thought I had to go slow but I did. This was my sweet Esme. My body ached with years of pent up need for her but I lifted my hands to her shoulders and forced them to stay put. No way would I allow myself to touch the rest of her. But we could kiss. I'd give her hundreds, thousands of kisses. I'd give her everything and anything she wanted. My eyes were shut but all I could see was Esme. I inhaled her, desperate to sink into her and devour. And damn it, yes, Esme was right there with me, giving me everything, so soft, so sexy, so hot. My need ate at me. I wanted more. I wanted her—now. My carefully constructed barriers were bursting open, my reasons for taking it slow falling by the wayside.

She scrambled closer, her heat searing my lap, her softness pressing against the rigid flesh straining to claim her after years without. My control was slipping fast, and in another minute I didn't know if I'd be able to stop. I jerked away, my breathing harsh and erratic, my body throbbing. And still, I didn't dare let my hands stray from her shoulders.

"Babe, you taste like birthday cake." I chuckled low in her ear. "But we're still in front of my parents' house."

"I don't care." Esme's sexy squirm against my hardened thighs almost undid me.

Jaw clenched, I found the self-control to lift her back into the passenger seat. "You should. I don't want our first time— your first time to be in a car. We better get going before Ivy shows up out here to investigate."

"Ivy wouldn't!" But still Esme dropped her arms from me fast, smoothing down the tee shirt that just couldn't seem to stay tucked in.

"She might." Since Chris died, Ivy had taken to mother-henning our entire family and all of her friends. "Best not give her a reason to walk outside." My hands shook so much it took me three tries to buckle my seatbelt. Lowering the window, I sucked in some cool, sanity inducing air as I adjusted in the seat as unobtrusively as possible. I'd been wound up with feelings for Esme for literal years. Finally, I get to kiss her and we're in a car in front of my parents' house? My aching body begged for relief. But we would wait.

A slow silent ten count later, I put the car in gear. I was preoccupied for most of the ride back, forcing logic to supplant the desire flooding my body. Esme focused on maintaining our connection. I didn't pull away when she covered the hand I rested on the console between us. Kissing her, just being with her after so long was surreal. Part of me fully expected to wake up any minute, rock hard with frustration and sheer disappointment, the way I had for years after dreams of her. So no, I wasn't about to deny myself the simple pleasure of her soft hand. Because that meant this was real. We were real.

After I slid the containers of risotto and birthday cake into the fridge, I checked my cell which had pinged with a slew of texts during our drive back to my place. Alex had organized the surveillance at Esme's apartment building. So far, no sign of her father, Gilberto, who according to Esme now went by the last name Garcia.

"I'm going to take a quick shower. I have work tomorrow." Esme clutched her bag of Target purchases under her arm.

"Esme, that's not a good idea. Everything's not one hundred in place. I'm thinking you should call in sick tomorrow. Give us a chance to finish setting up our people wherever we need them to be." What if Rojas knew where she worked? Surveillance had to be in place before I let her out of my sight. Even better would be if I could convince her to stay with me until that scum was behind bars.

Her jaw dropped. "I've never…"

I had to smile at her open mouthed shock at my suggestion. Esme was the quintessential good girl. "Never missed a day at work? Figures. One day of hooky is all I'm asking. Maybe two. Do me a favor and be vague. So you can take more time if you have to."

I don't think Esme realized she was squeezing the bag so tight its contents were spilling out onto the living room rug. "I've actually never taken a day off. Ever. I mean I'm healthy as an ox. Besides I like my job, not to mention, I need the money. I don't even take vacation days—just the pay."

Meeting her anxious gaze, I said, "A beautifully healthy ox who's very precious to me." I kept my voice even. "Babe, this is the safest place for you to be right now." I fished a burner phone out of the bottom drawer of the cabinet where I stored my weapon and put it on the counter. "You can use this to call your job or you can email them from my secure server."

I took the shopping bag and tossed it on the couch then covered her hands with mine. As fresh and gorgeous now as she was this morning, her lush lips still kiss-swollen, she looked lost in the middle of my living room. Here was a woman who'd studied and worked years to pay medical bills, her vocation contributing to society at the same time. Did she know she was the love of my life? Did she know I'd die before I let anything or anyone hurt her? Tenderness overwhelmed me as I unclipped the barrette holding her long hair, gathered and smoothed the tendrils that had escaped it and reclipped the whole thing. "You're taking care of me," she said in a tone of such surprise, I wondered how long it had been since anyone had.

"Always." My words came out low and rough and I stepped back. It was the only way to maintain any kind of concentration. "I'm conferencing with my team shortly. We'll come up with a workable plan to nab this dude. I promise, life will get back on course soon."

Esme chewed the corner of her mouth as she nodded. "I want to believe you're right."

"Count on it, babe," I said looking straight into her anxious emerald eyes.

CHAPTER 9

ESME

*A*LL I WANTED WAS to go back to my drama free life as a hospital researcher. But who was I kidding? Life would never be the same as long as I could still feel the debasing way Rojas pawed me in front of a room full of people like he had every right to. Like he owned me. My hands shook as I stripped off my clothes in Shane's bathroom. I needed to scrub the memory away. Again. I had to replace that flashback with the image of the only man I ever wanted to touch me. Shane.

I twisted my hair into a topknot and stepped into the shower, a nervous flutter ping ponging through my stomach at the thought of Shane, though he wasn't a thought or a memory anymore, he was a living, breathing, oh so tempting man. I'd finally admitted my feelings to him—feelings which, though bottled up, had been an essential part of me for more than half my life and now it was awkward. I was awkward. Shane and I had to navigate living here together for a couple of days with me having blabbed to his mom I'd "given my heart to him." Yuck, what a schoolgirl phrase. That was the truth of it though. I was a schoolgirl when I fell in love with

Shane. But now I was a woman with a woman's desires and a ton of lost time to make up for. Shane's response to my declaration was an epic kiss which made it clear I wasn't the only one who wanted, who desired. And yet, no answering words.

As much as it hurt to have my words hang in the air while Shane, without saying a thing in return, set off an avalanche of need inside me, to be honest, I was relieved. Because at least I said the words out loud. For years I wondered if I'd ever see Shane again. I'd finally made my peace with the idea it would never happen. But miraculously, we had met up again and I was glad I'd said it. No matter what, I was never going to deny my feelings for him again. And it seemed some people, like Clare, had me figured out all along.

The wine we all shared at Finn's birthday dinner loosened my tongue and Clare's welcoming acceptance of me opened my emotional floodgates. I always thought I hid my feelings pretty well but it seemed Clare could read my mind. Somehow, I'd opened up to her in a way I'd never been able to with my own mother.

Mama kept me hyper-focused on my studies, with good reason. There had been little time for female confidences or talk about crushes during my childhood. Even my quinceañera had been low-key, go out to dinner affair since we had no relatives in this country to invite to a birthday party and little money to spend on a celebration. Mama had preached and I had listened: head down, study hard, obtain an education—this was how an immigrant made her way up in the world. My mother was an educated woman. Back in Colombia, she'd been schooled in the classics, music, deportment. She'd done her best to pass on what she'd learned to me.

When she'd fallen in love with my father, an uneducated farmer, her family's shock had given way to sadness when we emigrated to America when I was five years old. By that time, my father had come up in the world, and now I knew how. He'd worked for Rojas as a drug courier. Had Mama known the source of his newfound wealth? Logic would dictate she should have. But then again my father's defining virtue was also his biggest fault. He loved Mama so much he would have done, and had done, anything for her. No doubt working for someone like Reinaldo Rojas meant he could provide for Mama in a way he felt she deserved. Did pride cause him to hide, or try to, the source of his improved financial security from her? Maybe Mama had discovered what he was doing to earn such money, maybe she encouraged him to break away from Rojas, and come to the states with Mama and me, escaping the life. In my recollection, Papá had always been a laborer here. Nothing more. He'd returned to the subsistence jobs of his youth, made his way in his new country as a law abiding man. There was something to be proud of in that. My father, poor but doing his best to work and care for his family without joining another branch of Rojas's army here in New York though the temptation surely was over-whelming.

I toweled off briskly, regretting the lack of my lotions and creams. I didn't even have lip balm. Pulling on Shane's sweats and tee shirt from last night, I examined my makeup-less features in his bathroom mirror. Ugh. Why had I chickened out of buying real pajamas in Target? No matter what I wanted, I wasn't about to drive anyone wild with lust in this get up. When I re-entered his living room, Shane was seated at the small alcove dining table hunched over his tablet. Though I was barefoot, he must have sensed my approach because he turned to me immediately, his mouth a tight, grim line.

"What's going on, Shane?" His shoulders could have been two boulders under his shirt, his fists tightening and loosening over and over but I would swear he had no idea he was doing it. He rose from his chair, took my hands, promptly let go of them, then strode into the living room raking both hands through his hair a half dozen times before he turned to face me again.

"Shane, what is it? You're scaring me. Is this about my father?"

"Yes. No. Not exactly." His words were clipped. He shook his head as if to clear it. "I don't wanna scare you. But this isn't playing out the way I wanted or expected. My superiors..." he took a breath, "we have to talk, Esme. I'm gonna need coffee or a beer or both." His laughter was hard and so unlike the light moments we'd shared at his parents' house, my stomach dropped.

"Then I'm gonna need a Fanta," I said and my words had the desired effect. Shane stopped in his tracks to rub a hand over stubble roughened chin and smile his Shane smile at me.

"Fanta it is, babe." He nodded me toward the couch as he went to the fridge. Shane ended up downing a quick espresso before he flipped the top off a bottle of beer. At my raised eyebrows, he said, "I know. I know. Don't judge." His beautiful lips curved as he ran a hand along the back of his neck, unable to find his words. I tried to relax my rigid spine in the corner of the couch but nothing about this situation or Shane's behavior eased my mind. I leaned toward him.

"Just *say* it," I insisted.

"Okay. They've gone up to the Powell and haven't spotted him there. Their idea is to use you to flush Rojas out from wherever he is." The words burst out of him in a violent rush.

Heat flashed up from my chest to scorch my cheeks as I stared at Shane because I knew where this was going. Finally I uttered, "how?"

"You'd wear a wire. They want you to...wear a wire." His

jaw hardened and he did that thing with his hair again till it was all standing on end.

I nodded quickly, my lips firming as I waited for him to continue. "Okay," I said.

"What? *Okay?* Esme, d'ya understand what they're asking you to do? It is not okay with me." Shane's voice shook louder with every syllable.

I kept my cool because he looked like he was about to jump out of his skin. "It's not okay with me. Nothing about this is okay. Even though I'm pissed as hell at him, I need to know my father's okay. I want to go back to my apartment, back to work. I want my life back. If the only way I can make it all normal again is by helping you get Rojas, I'll do it."

"You don't know what you're saying. You can't even bring yourself to say what he is. This guy isn't a jaywalker, Esme. He's a goddamned drug lord. The risks are…" he slashed his hand through the air, his eyes as turbulent as a storm-wrecked sea, "unacceptable."

"Shane. Remember last night? I know exactly what kind of garbage he is. I wish I could wipe it clean from my memory, but I can't." I scrambled over to straddle his lap. Scooched in till we were chest to chest looping my arms around his waist. I waited a beat while he stared at me, his face so stricken it might have been carved from stone. "Give me more information."

His hands came up to grip my elbows. "Esme, you seriously want to do this?"

"Yes. And I need you to explain it calmly so I can figure out what I'm letting myself in for."

He took an audible breath. "My superiors think and I agree, Rojas is now aware of the risks he took resurfacing in the city and he wants to get back down to Colombia asap. The Feds have him under indictment, there are warrants out for his arrest. So while he has every reason to want to get back to Colombia…they think Rojas may have enough interest in completing the transaction, to stay put here and give us the chance to grab him."

"The transaction?" I asked.

"You, Esme." His voice was brutal. "You're the transaction. They think he'll surface because he wants you. Now do you get why this is not okay?"

I swallowed but lifted my chin all the same. "What would I have to do?"

Shane's lips firmed into an unyielding line as he stared at me. Finally he spoke. "Basic plan is, you show up at your apartment. You'd call your dad first and tell him you're on your way because obviously Rojas was in contact with him when they set up the event that went down last night. You'd be wearing a wire. Wait for Rojas to appear. Engage him in conversation long enough for us to get to you. Like I said there are warrants, he's under indictment. So even if he doesn't admit anything about his criminal enterprise, as long as we know he's with you, we can converge and nab him." He clipped out the words, chest rising and falling with each angry breath.

"Sounds…" I swallowed the thickness clogging my throat searching for an upbeat tone.

"Don't you dare say easy." His voice was hard but the touch of his callused hands on my elbows was whisper light.

"And when do they want this to happen?"

"Tomorrow. We don't know if he'll skip out of the U.S. without us being aware like he did coming in. Or if he already has. Frankly, no one wants to admit we don't know exactly where he is right now. We're watching your place but so far no sign of him. But we're counting on his ego to want to resolve how you hoodwinked his handler and left last night. You'd be the…"

"Bait," I supplied.

"Yes." Shane's harsh breath eased out warm on my neck.

"Okay." If I needed a place to put my loathing of Rojas to work, this was it.

"Tomorrow, they, the officers in my squad, would come in an unmarked van to the garage downstairs. Female officer puts a wire on you, we brief you. That'll take less than two hours. You call your dad and then it's go time. You show up at your apartment and we wait to see if Rojas does too. After a few hours, if he doesn't show, that's it."

In spite of my bravado, my stomach churned tighter with each phrase he uttered. I was still on his lap and couldn't suppress the shiver rocketing up my spine.

"Esme. Look at me, babe." He tucked a tendril of my hair behind my ear. "You don't have to do this. I am not asking you to do this."

"I know."

"Do you? Or are you such a good girl you don't know how to say no?"

"Oh, you think I'm a good girl?" I tilted my head as I narrowed my gaze in on him.

"I know you are." He nodded sagely as he crossed his arms over his chest and I almost smacked him.

"You don't know everything, especially not everything about me, Shane Joseph Fortunato." I pursed my lips and raised an eyebrow. "We haven't seen or spoken with each other in ten years. Don't try to box me into your preconceived definitions of good and bad. I've made my choice." A pulse throbbed in Shane's jaw but he remained silent. "Enough about tomorrow," I said. "Let's talk about something else."

The relief on Shane's face was comical. "Okay. You know what I do. Tell me about your job. I remember a cute little kid with a braid and a lot of heavy books she actually read and understood everything about."

I chuckled. "Yeah. I'm a nerd. I admit it. My job? I guess most people would find it boring but I love it. Remember how I was always good at science?"

"You were good in every subject." His tone was a mixture of pride and envy.

"Yeah, well I really liked science. That together with my mom getting sick and I naturally gravitated toward a medical job. I'm a researcher at MSK. I work on a team with other research scientists, doctors, and technicians. We organize studies, execute them and analyze results. It's kind of tedious but exciting at the same time because you never know when something will click, when one of the therapies is the one that works. I love it. I feel like I'm making a difference, you know?"

"You're part of the team finding the cure. It's an important job."

"Like your job is."

He inclined his head saying, "I thought you didn't want to talk about that."

"I do. But not right now."

"Okay. What do you want to talk about?" He dragged out the words, wary of a subject change and why was this so difficult for me? Was I a good girl *and* a coward? In the car Shane kissed me like a man obsessed. Right now, I didn't want to talk about my career or his or tomorrow and what I knew I must do. Tonight would be for us.

"Let's talk about us. Just us. Tonight."

"Tonight?" He gritted out the word in a choked way and his Adam's apple moved as he swallowed.

I was still on his lap so I felt his whole body stiffen till he was rock hard and I mean his *whole* body. No doubt that's the reaction of any man with a woman sprawled on his lap but I didn't care. I'd press my advantage. Shane was the one for me. My only one. We were here, alone and I'd been given the gift of Shane, even if only for this one night.

"Yes, tonight. Us. Here. Alone." In spite of my inner bravado my voice retained its annoying huskiness and I was incapable of stringing together a complete sentence expressing my need. *C'mon, Esme. Don't lose this chance.*

Still, judging by his stricken expression, Shane got the gist. His big hands, which had been smoothing and cupping my elbows, stilled. "Esme. You don't know what you're asking."

"Yes, I do. But to the extent I don't? I want you to be the one to answer all my questions."

"Oh, babe…" His eyes squeezed shut and I couldn't tell. Was he unwilling or weakening?

I pursued my advantage. Literally moved in on him, pressing closer. "Shane, I want you to teach me. I want…you."

When his throat worked for endless seconds but he said nothing, I found the courage to lean in the smallest bit to taste the underside of his jaw. The groan he let out was other-worldly. And then he gave me what I wanted. Our lips collided and fused for an endless moment till Shane's tongue emerged to stroke the seam of my lips. I opened for him and he tugged me in, running one hand under the tee shirt from my hip to my ribs, then up farther till he covered one of my braless breasts with his warm, rough palm. His other hand moved up as well, but stayed on top of the thin cotton of the tee. The glorious friction of his thumbs flicking back and forth over the hardened points of my nipples shot pulses of searing heat straight to my core. Instinctively, I began to rock on his lap, my engorged breasts so sensitive I moaned into our kiss.

"Esme." Tonguing a wicked line from my ear to my throat, his uneven, gravelly voice made me shiver. "Feel what you do to me," he said, covering my hand and guiding it over the bulge behind his zipper. I sucked in a breath at his raspy words, feeling powerful with the hot weight of him under my hand.

"Shane," I pleaded, desperate to relieve the ache between my legs.

"Hang on." He pulled away, forcing me to focus on what he was saying. "Tell me something, babe. How far have you gone with this?" He glanced down at our bodies, a hair's breadth apart then back into my eyes. "Anything beyond kissing?" Lifting his hand, he smoothed the wisps of hair falling out of my barrette.

My words were caught in my dry throat. I shook my head no.

"And the kissing? Just on your lips?" He rubbed his thumb along my throbbing lower lip. This time I nodded yes.

"Okay." He sat back from me, breathing hard.

Okay? No, *not* okay. I wanted to shout and pound his chest. What was going on? "What did okay mean?"

"I needed to know. I don't wanna go too fast..."

"You're going too slow!" I gripped his biceps and squeezed.

A pained laugh escaped his mouth. "No, babe, if we do it right, there's no such thing as going too slow."

Dios mio. I sat back on my folded legs and crossed my arms over my chest. I was burning up and Shane was talking about slowing down.

"You look like an annoyed kid right now," he said with a half-smile.

"Shane! I'm not a kid anymore." Furious, frustrated tears loomed. "If you don't want to do this...just say so." I jumped to my feet and raced toward the bedroom, Shane's footsteps pounding fast behind me.

"Esme," he said to my back as I blinked tears away.

After a long beat, tears in check, I turned to confront him.

"You have no clue how hard it was for me to do that, to try to…come on to you, especially after what I said in the car before. If you don't want to do anything about it, please—" I turned away from him again, "—leave me alone," I said over my shoulder. My skin was burning with embarrassment and a healthy dose of anger.

"Esme. I'm sorry. I do want you. God knows, I do. Seems like I've spent my whole life wanting you. But I need to make it perfect for you." I felt his warmth behind me as his rough palm cupped my elbow. "Babe, can you look at me? I'm trying to apologize."

I turned to see his solemn gaze focused on my face, a splash of color staining his cheekbones.

"There's no way it won't be perfect for me, Shane. That's what I'm trying to tell you." I took a step toward him. "I just don't know what you want."

"You haven't made a wrong move yet." He lowered his head till his lips tickled my ear. "You turn me on so hard I can't think of anything else. I don't wanna go slow. But I have to make it good for you. Understand?"

To cover my blush at his gritty words, I waved a hand at the unglamorous tee and sweats. "Really?" I said.

"Yep," he said. "Even in those you look like a goddess."

"I waited for you, Shane. I didn't realize it but I was always waiting for you." I gripped the hem of the tee shirt, pulled it over my head and dropped it on the rug.

CHAPTER 10

SHANE

*E*SME SKIMMED the sweats down her thighs and stepped out of them. Then she stood in front of me, a small smile curving her lips—proud, defiant, nervous and all woman. I recognized the lacey white thong as one of the ones she teased me with when she bought them earlier today. "A goddess," I said again, the words rasping out of my dry throat. A deep rose suffused her skin and my body hardened in response. With care bordering on reverence, I rested my hands on her shoulders, allowing my thumbs to skate over the silken skin there. Esme pressed her body against mine, her breasts tormenting my chest, lithe thighs restless against mine. I promised myself sometime after our explosive kiss in my car, I'd go slow when all I wanted to do was rip our clothes off. A harsh breath escaped my tight throat as her fingers slid between us to rest on my chest then flicked open the buttons on my shirt. I left her to it as I tasted every inch of her neck. In between her soft gasps and quivers, her hands worked my belt buckle and opened the button of my jeans. I kicked my clothes off, then cupped Esme's jaw, tilting it up and covering her mouth with mine. *Mine.* I was the luckiest son-of-a on the planet. Esme was liquid fire in my arms and with her softness resting so trustingly against me, it was all I could do not to pound my chest and proclaim it to the world. Mine!

"You're mine, Esme." My arms tightened around her. My voice was harder, more possessive than I meant it to be. But I wouldn't deny it. "Once we do this, there's no going back. You understand?"

She rimmed her reddened lips with the tip of her tongue. "And you understand this, Shane. Same goes. *You're mine,*" she said.

Oh yeah. I was all in. This woman. *My* woman. I backed us toward the bed and yanked the quilt down. She started to scramble under the sheet. "Cold?" I asked. She chuckled out a nervous no. I planted a quick rough kiss on her mouth. "Don't worry, then. We won't be needing sheets or a blanket. I'm gonna keep you warm all night." I grabbed a condom from the bedside table and threw it on the mattress. Her eyes widened at the sight of it, a dusty rose coloring her cheekbones.

Then I lost myself showing Esme everything about how good it can be between a man and a woman. But not any man and any woman—us. Only us. How good it always would be between us.

I worshipped every inch of her skin starting with her lush lips, before moving to her flushed breasts, then skimming down her quivering belly, and her silky legs, planting lingering kisses on every scrape and bruise. My erection tormented me—and her, because I wouldn't let her touch it while I loved her. Because there was no way I'd last even one swipe of her hand, much less her mouth. When I reached the heart of her, she was practically vibrating, pleading with me to finish her.

"See how good I can make you feel?" I nuzzled between her thighs.

"Shane, you're making me crazy." She bucked and squirmed beneath me.

"Babe, I'm gonna make you feel even better. Let me. Only me." Gently I held her thighs open and feasted, her husky moans egging me on. When she shattered into her climax under my lips, I ripped the condom open and entered paradise.

The room was still dark when I was roused by Esme's hardened nipples stirring against my back, as her hand stroked my abs and feathered downward.

I sucked in a breath. "Looking for something?" I asked in a choked mutter.

"Just exploring," she said with a sleep husky laugh. Her hand teased lightly over me then tightened. "Ah, look what I found. Mi tesoro."

I'd learned a little Spanish in school, or tried to, but even I couldn't mistake her meaning and Esme didn't give me a second to puzzle over it anyway. Tension coiled my abs tight as her slender, knowing hands found me. I hissed in a strangled breath when she cupped me. Then she rose to her knees and planted a sultry kiss on my mouth as her hand continued to stroke my now rock hard erection. One kiss turned into another and Esme's breath puffed out in erratic bursts as her hips dipped and circled in response to my questing fingers. "Ready to give me another lesson, Shane?"

"Always ready for you, babe," I said on a grunt. "And I think you're ready, too." I'd wanted this woman for so long it might have been tough to separate Esme the dream from the two of us together in reality. Because this—right here, right now was the stuff of fantasy. But no way could Esme, so sweet, bold and warm in my arms, be compared to any daydream I could conjure. I wasn't capable of fantasizing real life Esme. She was my first love. Her name would be on my last breath. She was my anchor, my friend and at last, my lover. If she'd have me, I'd never let her go.

Grabbing protection from the drawer I hastily slid it on when Esme positioned her supple, pliant body astride me and leaned down for a soul-shattering kiss. I entered her with a groan and one barely controlled upward stroke. With both hands on her ass, I guided her movement to keep it slow and rhythmic, anything to prolong our pleasure. But the goddess in my arms wasn't having it. Esme set a faster pace, her knees clasping me tight at my torso, her breasts rosy and bobbing. We flew together on a level beyond speech, her moans and sighs, my grunts and groans the only sounds in the room until I chanted her name like a song. *Esmeralda!*

She collapsed on top of me in a warm huddle and I knew when my time came to die, this would be my go-to way to do it. With this perfect woman in my arms. I shook off the morbid edge of that thought. But it was tough to discard it completely because today was already here. I closed my eyes with my arms tight around the goddess still straddling me and we slept again.

Both of our phone alarms went off at five-thirty and the combined racket, apparently we both favored cymbals crashing over mellow birds chirping, had us bolting up together. Esme giggled as she scooted out of bed and ran into the bathroom before me.

I could get used to this.

The shower was still on after I gulped down a black coffee and I knew this was too good an opportunity to miss.

"Shane!" Esme's throaty shout dissolved into laughter as I stepped into the gray and white marble cubicle with her.

"Hey, c'mon, don't be a water hog," I said.

Esme swung a mean washcloth and hit my chest. "How can I hog the water when you're blocking the showerhead? Move over, you big…aahh…"

I really crowded her space then, and her soapy torso slid back and forth against mine in a lazy dance. In moments my length hardened and pointed home like a heat seeking missile. I stilled as the steaming water slid over us, willing my body into control. I couldn't take advantage of the situation. Esme should be resting, sleeping in my arms. She'd been a virgin till last night. But instead of spending the day alone in bed, we planned to be out of the apartment to meet my team within the hour. I tilted her chin up with a forefinger and pulled her in for a long kiss, then stepped out of the shower and grabbed a towel.

I popped English muffins in the toaster after I dressed. Gulping another coffee, I frowned as Esme left her muffin on the plate after taking two bites. "No time to show off my omelet making skills right now," I said. "But you should finish that." I nodded to the muffin.

She grabbed her middle. "Nah-uh. I can't stomach the idea of even a muffin today." She took one more desultory bite of the muffin then pushed it aside, pacing to the window.

"Yeah, same." My stomach twisted as I texted confirmation with my squad of our meeting place and objective.

Esme might look carefree in tight white jeans and a flowy green peasant blouse, courtesy of yesterday's trip to Target but I knew the signs of her unease. She'd always been reserved and observant, her serene smile her go-to way to help everyone around her feel comfortable. But there was such a thing as being too much of a people pleaser. Esme was capable. She could walk into her apartment today and handle whatever they threw at her through sheer force of will. But she had no training and no weapon and those were just two of the obvious, major disadvantages.

Fact was Rojas had out-maneuvered us more than once—and we were a joint federal, state and local law enforcement operation who'd already dedicated years to bring him to justice. So yeah he could do it again. And this time it wouldn't be some unlucky undercover operative whose life would be on the line. It would be the perfect, amazing woman who'd rocked my world last night and who I didn't want to let out of my sight for the rest of my life.

Her smile was determined and upbeat. Amazing to think she was trying to bolster my courage when the weight of this day and what it might bring lay heavy on both of us. I was immobilized. I didn't want to meet the wire team. How could I allow it? I'd just reconnected with her and already I was putting Esme in harm's way. It didn't matter what she agreed to, how much we both wanted to nab Rojas, today could go sideways in a million different ways. On a basic level I didn't want her anywhere near Reinaldo Rojas no matter what she said. Let them find another way to get to him.

"Esme, I've been..."

She held up two hands chest high. "Before you say whatever you want to say, tell me something. Why did you join the NYPD? I know you're the eldest in your family. I saw the way you took being the big brother so seriously when we were kids. I always admired that part of you. But why?"

"Esme, I could make a joke or we could get into a big

discussion but we don't have time right now. I'm gonna reach out and call the whole thing off…"

"First *tell* me, Shane. Why did you become a police officer?" She pinned me in place with an incisive look.

Damn. So long ago. It was all so long ago but sometimes, like now, the pain was as fresh and unexpected as the chill morning breeze drifting through the living room window. The phone call to my base in Iraq. My dad, my singing all the time, fun-loving, giant-sized, moving man of a father, sobbing in my ear telling me Christopher was gone with Ma, my sisters, and my brothers, all in tears in the background. Compassionate leave to attend the funeral, our family stunned with grief. Returning to finish out my hitch and the weight, the pressing necessity to do something—anything, to make the pain go away. The decision to attach value to our senseless loss.

The natural, to me anyway, decision to join the NYPD. Becoming a cop meant my grief had a purpose. Drugs killed Chris and as I climbed the ranks, I made my career chasing bad guys who moved drugs or dealt them in the city. I turned away from her probing gaze to close the window.

"Shane?" I didn't want to say a word but Esme's steady, patient voice soothed me into speech.

"Babe, I think you know why already. Because…it was because of Christopher. I couldn't…I wasn't there for him. I didn't help him." My gaze shifted from her too sympathetic eyes to my shoes. "He died and I should've been there for him." I said the words out loud. Words which had been part of my being since the moment I got the news. Words which had fueled my every action since then. My voice thickened but I wouldn't let the tears come. I hadn't ever cried for him. But my family's tears had cut me deep. Their tears told me I should have been there. I should have protected Chris. Instead, the one thing, the only thing I could do was put my grief to the one use I could find for it, eliminating the scourge and the scum of drugs and drug dealers from everywhere they lurked in my city.

"I'm not going to argue with you—right now—about what you think you didn't do for Chris, even though for God's sake Shane, you were overseas. Right now I just want to say you've made it your career to protect people from drugs and take whoever sells them off the streets. It's personal to you."

"Damn straight." She was tying me in knots. I didn't want this day. Esme couldn't be a part of this. But I hated to see that bastard slip away one more time.

"It's personal to me too, Shane. Chris was a friend of mine. And Reinaldo Rojas has a hold over my father—and me— I can't break until he's put away. I have just as much motivation to get him. My father, he's flawed... but after all is said and done, he's all I have. And I'm all he has now. Don't even think about calling this off. I'm all in. Tell me what I have to do. And then let's go get it done."

Her hand was tight on my forearm. My heart, my mind, my instincts, my training, all of it was at war inside me. Pain came at me from all sides: my past mistakes melding with the pain which would surely follow if I allowed Esme to come into contact with that monster. It couldn't happen.

"You don't know what you're saying yes to." How could I make her understand the risks were too great?

"I know I can't get back any kind of normal life until I, until we...deal with this."

"Babe, please. The stakes are too high. No question he'll be armed and his soldiers will be with him and armed too. Remember the dude who took your phone? He has dozens more like him."

"I remember everything. But this time I won't run. This time I'll agree, make him believe I've changed my mind, that I was nervous but now I'm...willing. That will give him a level of comfort and enough time for you and your team to respond."

I shook my head. "I hardly slept last night thinking about this."

"Me either. One way or another, neither of us got much sleep last night." She winked.

I slammed my palm on the quartz counter. "Fuck sake, Esme. Don't try to make anything about this funny. And I wanna tell you something else. You're wrong about something. Your father isn't all you have. Not by a long shot. You have me. You've always had me from the first day I met you. And you have my family. Don't ever forget that."

Her eyes filled but her chin firmed at the same time. She wouldn't let the tears come. Shaking back her hair, she said, "Shane, if I don't face this head on, I'll never move forward. Neither will you. Let's do this for us. And for Chris and my dad." She glanced up at the clock beside the fridge. "It's nearly seven. Let's go." She said it like it was just another work day.

CHAPTER 11

ESME

ONCE WE GOT out of the elevator at the garage level of Shane's building, I put on my lab coat so to speak, sliding into scientific observation mode as I absorbed my surroundings. Shane's usual easy smile had completely evaporated after our conversation and we walked in silence toward a white Econoline van, alone in a far corner of the garage, its side panel emblazoned with *Ed's Electric* in red script. He used one knuckle to tap lightly on the back door and it clicked open immediately.

I climbed awkwardly into the back of the van, my completely ridiculous, chosen to lure Rojas, heels and tight jeans hampering easy movement though Shane's hand, warm at the small of my back, steadied me. A wiry forty-something year old guy in cargo shorts and navy tee shirt, his dark frames perched on a prominent nose, straddled a stool and tapped a laptop. Huge headphones hung from a hook beside his makeshift desk which was actually a short panel of plastic jutting out from the inside wall of the van. The van's interior had been stripped of the usual rows of seats to accommodate another couple of stools in front of another two plastic makeshift desks while a bunch of orange and white tool cases, the kind electricians and other tradespeople use, were stacked in one corner. The guy wearing glasses turned in time to notice Shane's hand resting at my back and I took a sideways step away from Shane so he'd drop his hold. I thrust out my hand to him, saying, "Hi, I'm Esme." The guy pushed his glasses back up his nose. After a long moment and without a hint of friendliness, he put his hand out and said, "Detective Stuart Schmidt."

Another guy, tall as Shane, ducked his head and entered the small interior from the front of the van's driver's side. I recognized him vaguely from a couple of nights ago as the driver of the car Shane jumped out of when he reappeared in my life. As Shane greeted Detective Schmidt, the other man approached and said, "Alex Morales. Shane's partner." Alex looked to be about Shane's age, and had a similar look—longish hair curling at his collar, casual, rumpled jeans and tee shirt with an unbuttoned dress shirt over it. No doubt he'd concealed his weapon like Shane had and disguised both weapon and physique under the baggy street clothes.

"Pleased to meet you, Alex." My nerves were off the charts. I'd used what little bravado I possessed to convince Shane I was up to the challenge of the day. But I was so *not*. To hide my uneasiness, I smiled broadly, too broadly for the occasion and stuck my hand out again. Shane bristled behind me. At my friendliness? Really? *C'mon, Shane.* Too bad my very proper mama never taught me the appropriate behavior when being introduced to detectives before getting wired to bust a drug lord.

Stone-faced, Shane led me to one of the stools before barking at the two men. "Where's Sheila Collins?"

Alex answered. "She's on her way...coming off another assignment uptown. But we can get started if you're antsy..."

"We'll wait." Shane's jaw clenched hard on the words.

Alex lifted a placating palm. "Dude, let's use this time for the briefing." At Shane's infinitesimal nod, Alex outlined the plan.

"Okay, let's go over the likely scenarios for today. First, once you're mic'd up there's no need to think about the wire. Don't touch it. Best try to forget it's there. Detective Schmidt over here," he jerked his chin at the man, "his entire job is to listen to what's happening in the apartment. It's all of our jobs to keep you safe. Once Rojas gets there, if he gets there, the best way you can help is to keep him in the apartment as long as possible. Keep him talking, if you can. We get into position and take him. If at any time you're under duress and you can't get out of there the word is cat. Say something about a cat and we come in and get you."

"Cat? Okay. And here I thought bird was the word," I quipped with a forced smile. Morales guffawed and Schmidt cracked a half smile but Shane's rock-hard jaw didn't budge.

"Just remember, Esme. No matter what happens. We'll get to you. *I* will get you." Shane caught my gaze as he said it, his eyes so dark they looked black.

I held his look and firmed my chin just like he had. There was no way I'd show him my fear. What would be the point? My pseudo-confidence would inspire his. "Got it."

Alex continued his lengthy instructions till I was ready to scream. Yes, I was keyed up but my stress begged me to take action—do something concrete. Still I took some comfort from the fact it was clear Shane, Alex and the rest of team were well used to these operations, even though as they disclosed, they seldom had a civilian wearing the wire. That and the knowledge their partners on the federal side were also in the vicinity gave me a level of ease. They all knew what the hell was going on and what everyone should be doing. Another tap at the back door and a tall, athletic female hopped into the back of the van with a lot more grace than I'd been able to muster earlier.

"Good. Detective Collins, Sheila, this is Esme Acosta...er, Garcia. Sheila will get you fitted with the device." Shane stated the obvious, his face closed off and more expressionless by the second. My face heated as he fumbled over my father's current surname. I still went by Cabrera-Acosta. I'd always used Cabrera-Acosta in this country, which in traditional fashion was a combination of my parents' surnames. But my father continued to switch out our surname every year with every new apartment rental. With his network of friends we didn't need to sign our names or present ID to rent another apartment or sublet. All we had to do was pay in cash. But it hadn't mattered what my father did or what name he used. Rojas had found him so easily now I realized he must've known where we were every time we changed apartments. Rojas was toying with my father. And he'd decided our time for running was over. But we'd out-think him. We wouldn't try to flee to Texas or anywhere else. We stay here and help the law bring him to justice.

"Would it kill you to smile, Shane?" Detective Collins teased before shooing the men out of the van. She met my relieved look with a raised brow. "It's easier and faster if we don't have them hanging around making everything that much more awkward, ya know?" She gave me a swift appraisal, her tawny eyes sharp. "That gauzy top is a little too sheer. I have something you can put under it." She rummaged in her bag. "Here." She held up a black tank top. "Take off your blouse and we'll get started. Then you can put the tank on and the blouse over it and we'll see what we've got."

My hands shook as I fumbled with the buttons of my blouse and I blew out a long breath. Damn, I was only a few minutes into this thing. I had to get my nerves under control.

Detective Collins' touch was light and efficient. In under five minutes she secured the tiny wireless device to my skin under my bra line before standing back and fixing me again with a narrow-eyed once over. "It's natural to be tense. Use that to your advantage. The situation *is* nerve-wracking so your stress makes sense. You'll come off as believable which can only help because Rojas can suss out trouble the way mice smell cheese. Remember, we have your back. You're in extremely capable hands here. Especially your guy Shane. He's good people."

"He's, ah…" My face heated as I stumbled over how to concisely describe my relationship with Shane. I shrugged, unwilling to say more than, "Shane and I knew each other as kids."

"Not my business. Just a trained observer. I have a lot of confidence in him and you should too."

"I do." Shane would do his best to keep me safe. I knew that with my entire being. Even if we had no personal relationship, I was sure both his conscience and his oath meant he would do everything in his power to catch Rojas and keep me out of harm's way.

"Good. Have confidence in yourself, too. Put everything back on now and let's see how you look and if Stu Schmidt can hear."

The men lumbered back into the van and in a couple of minutes Detective Schmidt issued a thumbs up.

It was time.

Detective Schmidt handed me a cell phone and I tapped in the digits to my father's cell.

"Papá?"

"*Gracias a Dios, M'ija*, where have you been? I've been so worried about you."

"Are you home?"

"*Por supuesto*, Esmeralda. Where else would I be? Where are you?"

His words were marginally upbeat and yet he'd completely ignored the fact I'd told him not to go back to the apartment till he heard from me. But his voice was scratchy, drained, and all of the anger I carried against him for placing me square in Reinaldo Rojas' path disintegrated. Or most of it anyway. This was my father. Yes, he'd dragged me into this. I couldn't forget it and what hurt most was his inability to treat me as an equal—someone he could confide in. But I also couldn't forget everything he'd done was ultimately the result of his love for my mother. If I needed proof I was a distant second place to my mother in my father's affections, I had it. Truth was since I looked so much like her, I could guess how much it must hurt my father to see the living reminder of his lost love in me now she was gone. Knowing how I felt about Shane, how I lived every emotion he'd suffered and still suffers over Chris, I got it. When you love someone, he was on your mind, first thing in the morning and last thing as you closed your eyes at night. You dreamed about him. His pain was yours. He was your entire focus. I sucked in a deep breath. Everything would work out fine today. I loved Shane and my father enough to conquer my fear and do what I had to do.

"I stayed with a friend but I'm coming home now. See you in a little while."

As instructed, I signed off quickly, handed the cell back to Detective Schmidt and then the van was in motion. In the front passenger seat, Shane's gaze fixed straight ahead as we rumbled across town eastbound toward Delancey Street. There was no chatter. We were all absorbed in the task ahead. My stomach churned with the motion of the van as it bounced in and out of potholes, the nauseating up and down made worse by my inability to see out of the darkened windows.

Fifteen endless minutes later, Alex pulled into a commercial driveway close to my usual subway stop. Detective Schmidt turned to address us all from his position in front of his equipment. "No one has been seen entering or leaving the premises since Ms. Garcia's call," he said. I nodded. This was good news, right? Maybe Rojas and his soldiers hadn't been able to track me and my father. Shane turned then and stared at me, examining my face like he was trying to memorize it. I mashed my lips together against all the words I wanted to say, platitudes like *I got this* and *don't worry* coupled with private words of love. Truth was: I was scared shitless and damn— it better not show in my eyes. I lifted my chin as Shane strode toward me. When he was in front of me, without saying a word, he lifted one large hand to smooth the hair at the nape of my neck before he pressed his mouth to mine in a quick hard kiss. I had no time to react before he stepped back. Twin coins of red darkened his otherwise ashen face. I clambered out of the back of the van, his kiss still hot on my lips.

As I climbed the four flights to our apartment my heart hammered with increasing trepidation, interspersed with ever more forceful self-talk. *You can do this, Esme. You are the perfect person to handle this situation.* But the kind of pep talks that might suit a tricky work problem were entirely too tame for what I was about to face. I said a quick prayer to Mama to watch over us.

I put a hand to my roiling stomach before I called through the door. "Papá, it's me. I don't have my key." There was a shuffling sound and then the door was ajar with a few inches of my father's pasty face visible in the opening.

From inside, I heard the quick, low voiced Spanish query. "Who else is out there?"

"Nadie." No one, my father answered.

Then the door swung wide and I was faced with Reinaldo Rojas's handler, the jerk who took my phone. With one hand he grasped my forearm, yanked me inside the apartment and shut the door. It was then I saw the gun in his other hand. The gun was pressed to the back of my father's head behind his ear.

CHAPTER 12

ESME

*P*ABLO SCOWLED AT ME. The fact that his left eye was practically swollen shut and his left cheekbone sported an angry purple splotch against his sallow skin only increased the sick grind of my stomach. No need to guess why he looked at me like I was a bug he couldn't wait to squash. He paid the price for failing to stop my hasty departure from the hotel on Saturday. I returned his glare with as much ice as I could marshal, determined to project a confidence I didn't feel. I held up my free hand, palm out. "You can let go of my arm, *señor*. I'd like to kiss my father."

Pablo's smirk said he heard me but his only response was to increase his hold on my upper arm. In an awkward movement, still determined to emanate calm, I leaned toward my father and brushed my lips against his pale cheek. It was clammy against my lips. I forced a deep breath, searching for an authoritative tone. Showing my fear would do nothing to help me or my father. "I'm here now. Can you please take the gun away from his neck?"

He ignored my request reaching past me to engage the lock on the door. "You won't get away again," he said.

"No, I won't," I agreed, my gaze sweeping from his livid face to my father's pallid one. "Would you let him sit down? He needs to sit." In response his grip on my arm intensified and I let out an involuntary yelp.

"Pablo!" From the passageway that led to our small bathroom, a harsh voice barked the command and then Rojas himself stepped into the main area of our studio apartment. With two days growth of beard and wearing a paint spattered white coverall, he looked nothing like the bespoke suited magnate he portrayed at the hotel party. No need to guess how he'd eluded detection by whichever cops were watching the building.

This was important. Shane and his team needed to know. I forced a smile, like it was normal to see this criminal strolling around our small place like he owned it. "Señor Rojas. I almost didn't recognize you, dressed so..." I hesitated, not wanting to insult.

The señor advanced, puffing out his chest as he insinuated his body between me and Pablo, forcing Pablo to drop his iron grip on my arm.

"We are both..." his gaze lingered on my tight jeans, "informal today." He shrugged. "It is necessary for me. And you are—" his gaze skimmed over me again in a way that made my skin crawl—"lovely as always. But listen well." He raised an imperious finger. "You will not wear those again, *l'entiendes?* I'm a man and I prefer my women in dresses." He stroked a forefinger along my arm over the area where Pablo's fingers had left prominent red marks. "And..." he leaned toward me with an unholy gleam in his black eyes and fake whispered loud enough for Pablo and my father to hear, "if anyone marks you it will be me, and me alone."

I swallowed the bile rising to choke me. "As my husband," I said, my gaze dropping to the floor in what I hoped was a submissive manner.

"O mi puta," he replied. His whore. "Not every woman is worthy of marriage. And you have defied me once. I promised your poor Papá I would marry you because it was what he wanted to hear, *entiendes*? So much…easier to accept."

I knew better than to show emotion at the crude words uttered with such venom. My father might have balked if Rojas revealed he wanted me to be one of many women Rojas enjoyed. So, when Rojas said he wanted me as payment for our debt, Rojas sweetened the deal, and won my father's assistance getting me to the cocktail party, by saying he'd want me as his wife.

When I chanced another look at him, his glassy eyes got me wondering. Had he been snorting coke in the bathroom? Without warning he grabbed my elbow and yanked me into him. When our bodies touched, I failed to swallow my gasp and my wide-eyed glance at my father only enflamed him. "I'm happy you chose to come back here…to me, *querida*." His hot breath was heavy with onions. "It's true, no man likes a…" he moved closer, "romantic adventure more than me but you understand a man in my position cannot indulge in such behavior or permit it in a woman."

"I understand." I suppressed a flinch when his hands dropped to a tight clasp of my waist.

"Bien. Because it would not have gone well for you or your father if I had to wait another day for you to come to me." He lifted a forefinger to tap my cheekbone—hard. "But now you understand and you obey. You are a bright child. A scientist, no? Your father must be proud."

My father's shame shadowed his eyes. "I am very proud of my daughter." His subdued voice cracked.

Rojas nodded like a beneficent dictator. "Beautiful and brilliant. And a virgin. I am fortunate beyond measure." Rojas wet his lips with his thick tongue.

My face heated at his words and I outright shuddered at the idea of this nasty man touching me as Shane had.

No surprise he took my reaction as a boost to his ego. "A shy, blushing virgin." He laughed as he gripped the back of my neck. "I will enjoy showing you the ways of men." He looked around at our basically furnished apartment and focused on my twin bed with its bright turquoise coverlet pushed against the wall at right angles to the sofa my father slept on. "But not here." He grabbed the waistband of my jeans and jerked me toward him. "I told you, my woman will not wear such clothing." His impatience, the edge in his voice confirmed it. Rojas was high. He waved a hand at the small closet in the corner near the television, then pushed me from behind. "Find a dress, then we go."

Certain there was no way I could hide the revulsion that must be showing on my face I turned away quickly to the closet. *Keep it together, Esme. You can do this.* All I had to do was convince Rojas I was eager to go to Colombia with him in payment of my father's debt. All I had to do was go along for a short while. When we got outside Shane and his team would show up and Rojas would be arrested. I grabbed a full skirted yellow peasant dress off a hanger. It had sleeves and a high neckline. Modest and no chance he would see the recording device. Pablo blocked my path to the bathroom. "Excuse me, Pablo."

When his goon refused to move, Rojas called him off. "Imbecile. She will not go anywhere. It's a four story building and her father is here. That's right, isn't it, *querida*?" Rojas's flabby lips curved up at the endearment.

"Yes." I stood before him clasping the dress to my chest before I realized I was blocking the mic. I held the dress away from me pretending to shake out wrinkles.

Rojas pointed to the hallway. "You have two minutes. No

more. Then you will go with me, no matter if your Papá is dead or alive, *entiendes?*

I couldn't suppress the shudder that slithered down my back at his taunt and his satisfaction at my reaction was the nasty gleam in his eyes. "I understand," I said before I beelined to the bathroom, shut the door and started stripping, murmuring as I changed. "Rojas has a scruffy beard, he's wearing a white painter's coverall. I didn't see a weapon but the overalls are loose. Pablo has a mustache, a shiner on his eye, a black suit, and a handgun. I see the outline of another weapon under his jacket. I'm wearing a yellow dress. My father looks bad. He might've had a heart attack." I struggled to keep my voice matter of fact as I worked the small pearlized buttons going up the bodice of the dress. As I completed the last one at my throat I glanced at myself in the medicine cabinet's mirror. My cheekbones were flushed and my clammy hands shook as I shoved my hair back with one of the headbands I kept under the sink and left the bathroom.

"*Que linda*, Esmeralda. Better. In such a dress, you look very much like your mother." *My mother? Rojas knew my mother?* With that cryptic comment Rojas gripped my chin with hard fingers as his gaze moved at a snail's pace over my features and the snug fabric of the bodice. The contents of my stomach threatened to spill out of my throat even as I forced the words from my lips.

"Thank you, señor."

"We'll go now. The jet awaits us."

"Jet?" I hoped Rojas thought I sounded like a woman thrilled at the prospect of a vacation though I heard the hysterical edge to my voice. "My first plane trip." We'd arrived in the U.S. via passenger ship.

"I have much to show you then. In due time, of course." His eyes gleamed but then he frowned as he rubbed the cotton of my flowy skirt between his fingers like a buyer testing sub-par quality of the fabric. Like I was a piece of furniture. A possession found wanting.

"We will spend all of our time in Colombia?" Again I tried to imbue my voice with the eagerness of a woman anticipating a new, luxurious life.

"I do manage to travel sometimes." His harsh laugh displayed all of his prominent, gray tinged teeth. "I have many people in many places whom I pay to be discreet about my movements. But you will remain in Colombia, *querida*."

"I should pack some clothes now." I turned toward my closet with its suitcase on the shelf. Packing, even my meager wardrobe, would buy time anyway.

In response Rojas laughed so hard his face turned a mottled red. "Clothing? If you wear clothes at all, they will not be these rags. Come along. My patience runs low."

We were at the door. Rojas shoved a Mets ball cap on his head then grabbed my hand in one of his and reached for the doorknob with the other.

"Señor. Please. My father. I would like to say goodbye to him." With Rojas still clasping my hand, I turned to my father, alarmed at his compliant demeanor, masking my distress that his pallor had taken on a gray hue as he hunched on the stool near the kitchenette. I leaned toward him, enfolding his back and shoulders in my arms. He didn't return my embrace.

"Papá." I kissed his cheek. "I love you. Don't worry about anything." Conscious of my audience I continued. "I'm happy to go with Señor Rojas. He's an important man. I know he will treat me well." I turned back to Rojas and Pablo. "My father needs medical attention. Can you please bring him to the hospital?"

Rojas waved a dismissive hand. "No. When we depart American airspace I will allow it. Until then, he waits." His hand tightened on mine. "So now you have found your motivation to go, eh? And quickly." I looked over my shoulder at my father's defeated expression as Rojas yanked me through the door.

Once we were on the stairwell landing, his grip on my hand tightened further, the crested rings on his fingers digging into my skin till I thought my fingers might break. "Ow, señor!"

"You will become accustomed to my touch," he said, dragging me down the stairs so fast I stumbled in my heels. "Pablo has his instructions. And he learned his lesson after Saturday night. If anything goes wrong today your father will not live through the night. For that matter, neither will Pablo."

I swallowed the helpless rage rising in my throat. "Señor, nothing will go wrong but as you can see, he's ill. He's my father, I..."

"Your father promised you to me. A fair exchange for his debt. A beautiful, spirited virgin to grace my home."

I changed tacks. "I confess, if my father was not so ill I would be nothing but happy at the idea." I tried to inject girlish enthusiasm into my voice. "How many hours is the trip?"

"Long enough for you to get to know me very well. And *querida*, it is of no concern to me whether you are happy. Your happiness is nothing to me." He said it casually, his tone as cold and dead as his eyes, his grip on my hand punishing as we powered down the last staircase.

I swallowed the baseball sized lump of fear blocking my airway, not allowing myself to think, all my concentration on not falling down the last few stairs. But I had to keep talking. Shane and the team needed as much information as I could give them. "You have a private plane?" I sputtered.

"*Por supuesto*. A private jet. Today it's at LaGuardia but," he shrugged, "I move it often. One cannot be too careful in my

119

business as you must appreciate." Truly it freaked me out he could be coldly callous in one moment and conversational the next. Whether it was cocaine or a personality disorder didn't matter, his mood swings jacked up my tension even more.

When the grimy beige walls of the ground floor came into view I sucked in a welcome breath. "Yes," I said, as never breaking stride, he towed me along toward the front door. *Was this really happening?* Outside, in the city, beyond the tiny decrepit vestibule, the sun shone obscenely bright. For everyone else on this block it was a cool, clear, late spring Monday with the promise of summer in the air. For me and my father, our world could be ending. *No.* I wouldn't let myself go down the path of doubt. What could I do besides stay strong and complete this task? Shane and his team heard everything. They were outside waiting and Rojas would be arrested in moments. And please *Dios*, my father would survive this horror show.

After peering through the smudged, paint flecked pane glass of the outer door, Rojas pulled me into the alcove under the staircase. He reached into his pocket and in one menacing motion, flicked open a switchblade and raised it till it grazed the skin under my chin. "Listen closely. You walk with me. You say nothing. Pablo is watching. If anything happens to me your dear *papá* is dead. Make no mistake, no matter how beautiful you are, I will not hesitate to use this on you. I grew up in the slums of Bogotá. I'm not some poor *campesino* like your father. Do not test me."

"I...I won't." Damn, but I couldn't disguise the tremor in my voice. What did I pray for now? For my father's sake that Rojas escape back to Colombia? With me? Thick, oily bile surged to the back of my throat. I pressed my lips together and raised my chin. No. This would be over soon. I had done my part. Shane and the other cops would do theirs.

He opened the outer door and then I staggered down the cement steps in Rojas's wake, blinking as my eyes adjusted to the dazzle of the sunlight. I endeavored, as much as Rojas's gait would allow, to scan the street. Shane and his team had to be in position. The mic I wore was tested and retested. They knew my apartment, my building, everything they needed to know. I shielded my eyes searching the pavement but Rojas moved fast, scattering dawdling pigeons on the sidewalk, all kinetic energy, right hand in his switchblade pocket, the other yanking me along by my elbow. Halfway down the block he stepped off the curb, pulling me toward a double parked, idling black Cadillac. He tapped once on the tinted glass. The driver jumped out to open the passenger door blabbering an apology in Spanish for not seeing us approach. Rojas waved me into the back seat then slid in beside me. Another tap on the plexiglass separating the front from the back seat with his yellow gold crested pinkie ring and the vehicle sprang to life and shot down the street. Was this actually happening? Was I really on my way to LaGuardia with Reinaldo Rojas about to get on a jet bound for Colombia? Where was Shane?

CHAPTER 13

SHANE

I PACED the small interior of the van resisting the urge to rip off the damn headphones. But I couldn't because they were my only connection to Esme. I was following fucking orders and Esme was with Rojas following his orders. She was on her way to LaGuardia to board a jet bound for Colombia. *Ah, fuck. FUCK. Esme. Babe. I'm sorry. This is all my fault. It was never supposed to go down this way.* My gut warned me from the get-go this plan sucked. Esme should've never had to breathe the same filthy air as that scum no matter what the reason. When I heard her practically begging for her father's life, yelping in pain and saying yes sir, no sir to Reinaldo fucking Rojas, I lost my shit.

When I sprang out of my seat to punch the steel wall of the van, Stu Schmidt looked me up and down then ordered me to keep my head on straight. We'd been sitting side by side, Esme's every sharp indrawn breath broadcast like she was right here next to me. Except she wasn't. She was heading to LaGuardia with a monster and I was helpless. I was set, ready to bust down doors but the effing NYPD brass in their infinite wisdom, set up their plan with the Feds and I was not included. Alex, my partner had liaised with the Fed team and word came down I was charged with staying put. Had someone noticed and reported the connection between me and Esme? Was I left behind because they worried I'd blow the operation? My heart choked my throat. I couldn't swallow back the foreboding. Something went wrong. The plan wasn't supposed to play out this way. All I knew was— I knew nothing. It all went sideways and I was in the dark. Would I be left to listen in as Esme was violated by a criminal and I did nothing? Not in this lifetime.

I squeezed the back of my neck but there was no loosening the log crushing my shoulders or the boulder in my throat.

Another minute. That was all. Then all bets were off. I didn't know why things weren't going as planned but I couldn't help Esme sitting here. An image swam before my eyes. It was Christopher. He was in high school, sitting at a desk in the room he shared with Finn, hunched over some big books, studying for a test. I came into their room to tell him I enlisted. His face fell before he recovered. He tipped his chin up to grace me with his knowing smile. When he congratulated me he sounded mature and so much older than sixteen. I was never the student he was so he knew it was the right move for me. He said he'd miss me. I'll miss you too, bro, I said.

I scrubbed my palm over my face. No. That was not how today was gonna go down. No fuckin' last goodbyes. My woman needed me. I didn't care anymore. They could take my shield over this. They probably would and I just didn't care. God or grace or karma had brought her back into my life and I wouldn't lose her. Not now when I'd loved her for so long. There was no life for me without Esme. If she was safe I didn't give a flyer about anything else.

It was five minutes since she drove off with that scum.

Where was the team? What in holy hell was going on? Time was up. I had to get to her. I threw the headphones on the console. Stu jerked his head up, startled. I strode toward the driver's seat and turned to him.

"Bro, I'm following them to the airport. You can hop out now or come along for the ride."

"You lookin' to be a hero could get me killed, Fortunato. When a cop has a personal interest in a witness, mistakes get made. We have orders." Stu's tone was flat. Calm.

"Listen, Stu, I respect what you do with this…" I waved my hand at the electronics and computer shit he sat in front of. "But I'm not gonna be listening in, helpless from miles away when that creep puts hands on her when they're on a plane headed to South America. I'm not gonna be listening to his reaction when he realizes she's wearing a wire. Not happening. You tell them you hopped out to take a leak and I drove off. Tell them whatever. *I don't care.*" I climbed into the driver's seat, saying over my shoulder. "Put the live feed on so I can hear what's happening from up here."

Esme

THE ENTRANCE to LaGuardia was a maze of detour signs and orange cones. Rojas was cursing at the driver who was ensnared in the chaos along with scores of other unlucky vehicles. The driver leaned on the horn just like the rest of the drivers scooting from lane to lane on the four lane roadway like so many ants running toward a sliver of candy, the candy in this case being the fastest track to the correct terminal.

"I guess in New York City it would be handy to have a helicopter to get to your jet," I said, my lame joke a conscious effort to clue Shane and his team into where I was. If they're still even listening. I had to believe they were. I believed in Shane. But something wasn't right. And all I knew was I was one hundred percent certain if I got on a plane with Rojas I'd never see Shane or my father again. When I saw the driver bypass the terminal with flights to Colombia, I was puzzled. "Did we miss the terminal? We just passed Terminal Three...?" How would the team find me if I didn't tell them where I was? Was there a homing device embedded in the mic? Is spite of all the possible scenarios and instructions Alex Morales and Sheila Collins gave me, I couldn't recall. Damn, I was so nervous I couldn't remember half of what they'd told me right now. *Concentrate!* If I couldn't remember I had to assume they needed me to give them the information.

"You're very curious, aren't you, *querida*? I promise you I know where I'm going even if this imbecile, Jorge is confused."

"But..."

"Patience." He tapped my cheekbone with his knuckle and I drew a sharp breath at the pain. "I told you my jet is waiting. We access a very private area at the back of Terminal Three via Terminal Four."

I nodded like an eager pupil hoping those details were heard by the right ears. "I've never been on a plane before. Is yours like the ones I've seen in the movies? Does it have a television screen?" Playing up my ignorance about plane travel might flatter Rojas into revealing important details.

Rojas laughed so hard spittle flew from his mouth. "*Exactamente.* My Gulfstream has a big screen television, WIFI, dining area and... a bed. Indeed, it is bigger than the hovel you were living in. Which should make the trip to Cartagena most enjoyable." He slid closer to me on the leather seat and when his thigh brushed mine the small amount of food in my stomach curdled. How could I let Rojas assault me? How would I be able to stop him? And if he did, what would happen when he discovered the microphone? And when he realized I was no longer innocent? *Stop, Esme. Concentrate on now.*

I folded my hands primly on my lap and unclenched my jaw to speak. "Señor. You..." I pushed out a slow breath before speaking so my voice would emerge strong and serene. "My father told me we would be married before you...before we..." I couldn't make myself think it, much less say it. I was trying to throw any roadblock in front of his plans in spite of what he'd said in the apartment. Rojas didn't wait for me to find my words.

"Your father told you wrong." He clicked his tongue in fake dismay. "It's a shame to mislead an innocent. But in this case he did not lie to you. I lied to him to push my plans along. There will be no marriage." I felt my skin heat. "Ah, the blush again. You are almost as beautiful as your mother, Esmeralda."

"I didn't know you knew my mother."

"Ah, yes, your mother Gloria was known from Bogota to Cartagena, a rare beauty from an important family. She could have married anyone. *Anyone!*" His voice was charged with venom. "But she was a mere woman. Who did she choose? Bah. Your blasted papá, a man so poor, so proud and so stupid he refused to accept help from her wealthy family. Bah," he said again. "She was taken from this world too soon. And your father could do nothing to provide for her treatment. I knew everything. I saw everything. And I stepped in to help...when I judged the moment to be right. And your father was grateful, so grateful he asked how he could ever repay me for the loan. So now he pays, *entiendes*, with you.

His loss is my gain. I didn't win Gloria but at least I have her daughter."

My jaw tightened at his vicious smile and I had to turn toward my window to hide my disgust and quell my burgeoning fear. His recounting of my parents' relationship was close enough to what I knew to be the truth. My parents left their home country looking forward to a new future in New York but it was clear their pasts had followed them here. And my father was still the same stubborn, proud man he must have been as a youth. Rojas had kept eyes on us the entire time my parents and I lived in New York, swooping in when we were at our lowest. It was all so very nasty. We were nothing more than helpless blobs under Rojas's microscope.

The car was slowing, weaving its way around to an alternate entrance near Terminal Four. Shane wasn't here. No one was. I had to face the fact he might not get here in time. His frustration clawed at me. He wanted to be here but for whatever reason the plan was an epic fail. If I didn't want to be trapped in Cartagena come tomorrow, I had deal with the situation by myself. I was on my own.

I flinched when the zing of a zipper broke into my turbulent thoughts. Rojas was shucking the painter's coverall and kicking it away toward my feet. Thinking fast I turned back to my window as I surreptitiously slipped off my stilettos. In the window's reflection I saw Rojas tug a wind breaker from a small duffle hanging from the driver's headrest as he argued with the driver about the best approach to reach the jet in the distance. My heartbeat galloped forward when he removed a handgun from the duffle. Best to assume the driver was armed too.

Two men had lethal weapons and all I was armed with were stilettos? Oh God, no. *Think, Esme.* No...there was a switchblade. I could swear Rojas hadn't removed it from the pocket of the coverall. And now it would be mine. Rojas wasn't the only one who could brag about knowing how to use a blade. I'd bought one from a hardware store way back in eighth grade when my maturing figure caused me unwanted attention from the boys at school and men on the street. When my parents discovered my purchase they were so alarmed they called The Convent of the Sacred Heart and enrolled me the same day. I hadn't gotten rid of the switchblade though. I'd hidden it till I could figure out how to use it. There was only one person I trusted to help me out then—and now. Shane. He'd taught me what he knew and I was proficient. My blade now lay useless under my mattress. But if I could get my hands on the one in the pocket of the clothing at my feet, it could even my odds a bit.

As the car slowed Rojas tucked his gun into his jacket pocket as he continued to hassle the driver, micro-criticizing everything about the trip. When he turned to me I glanced up in a pretended flutter. "I have to slip on my shoes." I held up one of my stilettos and Rojas slashed an impatient hand. "*Subito,*" he said. He turned away from me as the vehicle glided to a halt and Jorge scrambled out of the car to open the passenger door on his side.

I released my seatbelt and bent double, sweeping my fingers over the discarded overall searching for the telltale outline of the switchblade while sliding on my shoe. There! I slid it out of the pocket, palmed it then slid it into the bracelet cuff of my long sleeved peasant dress in one motion. Sliding on the second shoe, I stalled for time. No way did I want to leave the relative safety of the car to board Rojas's jet. He peered into the car again then actually clapped his hands to hurry me along.

I climbed out of the car into sunshine even brighter than earlier. The sun was directly overhead as it was now almost noon. It seemed like another lifetime instead of mere hours ago Shane and I awakened together after the most amazing night of my life. *Focus, Esme.* I scanned the area best I could without sunglasses trying to determine whether anyone had noticed our trek out to where the silver jet sat about a football field away. But I saw no one. Just like there'd been no one outside of my apartment. Drawing audible breaths to squash my rising panic, I walked as slowly as I dared behind Rojas. Every few strides he urged me along with a string of imperious curse words as I did my best to review my options. Did I even have any? NYPD wanted Rojas. Supposedly the Feds did too. But here he was and here I was with nary a cop in sight.

At fifty feet way I was close enough to see the jet's door open at the top of a metal staircase. Jorge, Rojas's driver ascended the stairs first with Rojas's bag and disappeared to the right toward the main cabin. I climbed awkwardly, my cursed stilettos catching every other step on the grooved aluminum. The pilot came out to greet Rojas reviewing the weather report in rapid Spanish. It was projected to stay clear and bright for entire five hour flight time.

"Esmeralda." Rojas's voice boomed as he grabbed my hand in a punishing grip and tugged me forward. "This is Juan Rincon, my pilot." He introduced me as his woman. Everyone was a possession to Rojas: driver, pilot, woman, jet.

"Encantado," I replied. Then Rojas all but shoved me behind him toward the back of the jet while he continued his conversation with the pilot, boasting about his hotel in New York, his home in Cartagena and me. The pilot ate up every word or pretended to, even laughing uproariously at Rojas's disgusting joke featuring a trio of naked women, a bull, and a bear, uncaring I could understand every word. In spite of their offensive banter I took only a couple of steps into the interior of the jet heeding an urgency to remain near the front door. While it was open I had some means of escape.

The driver, Jorge approached me after delivering Rojas's

luggage to the back of the plane. He leaned forward slightly. "Do you need to use the restroom?"

"What?" I'd never been on an aircraft before much less used a bathroom on one. He caught my gaze and nodded once. "You need to use the restroom." He made it a statement and his intent gaze told me he wanted me to say yes. Something in his eyes made me want to trust him—but I couldn't.

"When you use the restroom, you should take care to lock the door. Shall I show you?" This man was trying to give me a message and I was ready to hear anything that could get me out of here.

"Okay sure." I followed him, trepidation in every step as he moved to the back of the plane. He opened the narrow lavatory door. Then he pointed at the lock and I could see either his limited command of English or plain fear of Rojas was giving him brain freeze. I lowered my voice to a whisper and spoke in Spanish. "What are you trying to tell me?"

He pointed to the sliding lock and demonstrated. "See?" he said in Spanish. Once you slide it, no one can get in." He was giving me a means of escape from Rojas while I was on the plane. If you could call it escape if I had to stay in the tiny lavatory with Rojas no doubt pounding on the door or worse, shooting the lock off to force me out. Hell no, there's no way I'd hide in the bathroom but damn, his stricken eyes told me he knew I'd want to lock myself into the lavatory rather than deal with Rojas once we were in the air. How many times had he been witness to Rojas doing whatever he damn pleased with a woman on his private jet?

This could not be happening. *Think, Esme.* I remembered something my father always said while my mother suffered through her final illness. While there is life, there is hope. We hoped for a cure while we all fought Mama's illness. I had to fight. In the front of the jet I heard another voice, the arrival of another man, introductions and pleasantries exchanged.

This was the second pilot. The jet would take off now. Time had run out. I had to get out now. Forcing down my panic, I evaluated my surroundings comparing this interior to what I'd seen on TV. By any measure, this jet was exceptional, perfectly spotless, with gleaming chrome or was it aluminum, lush carpet and rich caramel leather seats.

My gaze caught the discreet sign for an emergency exit near the window. No, not near the window. The exit *was* the window. My heart, already pounding a furious drumbeat, almost drowned out the sounds around me and accelerated painfully as I evaluated my means of escape. This was it. I wouldn't get a better chance.

I kicked off my stupid stilettos and as he watched my shoes fly under the seat, Jorge stepped forward speaking in an urgent undertone. "Señorita...!"

In seconds I had the switchblade in my palm. I flicked it open. "Try to stop me and I'll use this on you. Maybe you should use the bathroom so the señor won't blame you when I go. If you really have a brain you'll call 911 instead." His face blanched then flamed but I had no time to see what he'd do. I pushed the blade back up my sleeve, gathered the skirt of my dress in one hand and crouched on the seat near the wall. "Senorita, please! Listen." The driver's staccato voice was panicky but insistent. "There is another way out."

Shane

FOLLOWING ESME'S description best I could, I wound around the outskirts of Terminal Four. Back in the surveillance van, as soon as Rojas bragged about his ride, I'd searched online for a picture of a Gulfstream. Now I scanned the aircraft in my sightline hunting for a Gulfstream sitting on its own. A jet like that wasn't an everyday sight, was it? But fuck me if Rojas's jet was sitting in a field of identical jets. It helped nothing and no one LaGuardia Airport was always in renovation mode, with masses of confused drivers bumping along in vehicles alternately speeding up and stopping short in the rutted roads. The noise was hellish. Without Stu, I had no way to track Esme's position via the chip in her mic. I was struggling to hear her as it was with the air traffic controllers' domination of the air waves. All I had were two earbuds, less obtrusive but also less effective than the noise cancelling headphones we wore earlier. Stu hooked me up with them—his eyes all apology before he hopped out of the van in Esme's neighborhood. Who could blame him? Easier to tell our superiors I went rogue. Easier for him not to risk his neck or his pension so close to retirement.

Damn everything and everyone if they'd taken off already, I'd lose my mind. I pushed past the useless thinking to focus fully on the task at hand. Years of training and my unwavering desire to find Esme surged through me. Fuck, I didn't even care if I got Rojas now, as long as I got Esme back.

Esme's voice was muffled. She was saying something about putting her shoes on and Rojas was hurrying her along. *Good, Esme. Delay. I will get to you, babe.* Which had to mean they'd arrived. Driving fast but not so fast I'd miss them, I scanned the road ahead and to the sides of me, as well as the parking areas and stretches of runway in the distance. So many cars. But there were no Gulfstreams around Terminals Three and Four. Sweat ran a river down my back as a bus blocked my sightline for a half minute. I resisted the urge to lean on my horn like everyone else because with my luck, a uniform would stop me and explaining myself was a delay I couldn't afford.

Traffic was still crawling as I passed an outdoor parking zone, where all on its own, an old-school, black, Cadillac situated beyond the parking lot rumbled to the middle of the takeoff area before it slowed to a stop, near a Gulfstream farther out in the distance. The driver emerged, pulled open the passenger door. Out stepped the piece of crap, Rojas. Bingo. Much as I was desperate for a glimpse of her face, I didn't wait to see Esme. I concentrated on finding the way in to where they were so I could get close. I ditched the van and thank fuck the earbuds were still picking up the conversation. I hopped a chain link fence between the parking area and the secret runway, wondering how high up Rojas's connections went if he could park a jet in plain sight at LaGuardia with full confidence no one would disturb him. When I finally put eyes on them again there was no Esme. Two figures lingered at the doorway of the jet, Rojas and presumably the pilot.

I got closer, crouching behind Rojas's Caddy when I confirmed it was empty. In my ear Esme was speaking to someone, her voice low, saying something about a lavatory. I hear the impatience in her voice, and the underlying tension in her words was a livewire to my gut. Rojas was still in sight yammering to the pilot.

Then Esme threatened whoever she was speaking to and before I could make sense of what she said the emergency hatch at the back of the plane opened and Esme climbed out of the jet and thank fuck, ran like the athlete she is, to hide behind the jet's tail.

I backed up fast in her direction, weapon drawn, determined to block her from view and jesus fuck she was taking a switchblade to one of the tires near the tail. Who knew if a mere switchblade could puncture a tire but damn, I was proud of her ingenuity.

I don't know if Rojas heard the commotion or saw her bright dress, but he stepped onto the first step of the jet's staircase, pulled a weapon from his pocket and started waving it around while he shouted like a madman. I took aim but I was moving toward him and my shot pinged off the staircase. I repositioned myself to block any shot from reaching Esme then took better aim at Rojas. I got off a couple of shots and at least one hit the mark because he stumbled against the handrail and grabbed at his thigh. Then he lifted another weapon. A semi-automatic. He sprayed fire, indifferent to the bullets ricocheting off the jet and shit now he was stagger-walking down a couple of steps. I got off another shot as he took aim at me. I hit him in his hand this time. Good. Please God, don't let him get to her. He swayed on the stairs and the semi-automatic fell from his hand. I took a chance and moved even closer not sure how bad he was hit but I was still good. With one bullet left I raised my arm and took aim but fuck— he reached for the handgun in his jacket. Did he even have any bullets left in it? Guessing no, I stepped closer and fired. My shot hit the mark, his lower extremity but I couldn't see exactly where I got him because I went down.

My left shoulder burned with a white hot fire that radiated from my chest to my neck. Esme screamed my name in my ears.

EPILOGUE

SHANE

MY WATCH SAID four o'clock but who could tell if it was day or night with the blinds drawn? I shifted again trying to slide into a sitting position but it was difficult to pull myself upright and I was tired of lying prone. The hospital issue waterproof mattress made me sweat even more than I already was from the meds, on top of which I was wearing a God-awful hospital gown so it was impossible to get comfortable. Sleep wasn't happening.

I needed Esme here. Or rather I had to get out of here so we could go back to my apartment—alone. It's been two days and we're still surrounded by people. And not just family. The room's been swarming with NYPD brass and investigators. Thank God and all the saints as Ma would say, for body armor because only one bullet from Rojas's handgun made contact with my flesh and thank fuck, according to my doctor, it only skimmed my collar bone before lodging in a fleshy part of my shoulder. More luck. New York surgeons are the finest in the world in my humble opinion and the operation to remove the bullet was a success. Ironic. I'd come home from Iraq with nary a scratch only to get shot up in the line of duty at home. So when were they going to discharge me?

Rojas, the slimy turd, had also been wearing a bulletproof vest but I'd managed a good angle on him from my position on the tarmac and one of my bullets got him in his gun hand, the other put a hole in his thigh, nicking an artery. He was recovering from his wounds in a downstate prison hospital ward. The sleaze apparently had nine lives. The doc said anyone else would've bled out right there on the runway before help, summoned by of all people, Rojas's driver, arrived.

So yeah, I'm bruised and banged up but I'm here, alive and getting better every day. Esme's been living over at Ma and Pop's place for now. That she agreed willingly and hadn't insisted she'd be okay at her place or even mine, spoke volumes about how shaken she was by what went down at the airport. Whether she admitted it or not, she needed family around her right now and they were all there for her. She slipped right back into our big family again. God knows, she's always been the best part of me. But damn, I wanted her here.

A minute later she popped her head inside the door and a huge grin split my face. "Hey, babe. Thanks for coming. How's your dad?" Her father occupied another bed in this hospital.

"Shane, you don't need to thank me." She strode to the side of the bed and grasped my hands tight and I admit it, I was needy. I craved her touch, her words. "There's nowhere else I'd rather be than here with you. As for Papá, his doctor said he'll be discharged tomorrow."

"Lucky dude."

"Really lucky. And, your mom has graciously allowed him to stay at your family home for a few days."

"Good." I was happy Esme's old man was deemed well enough after his heart attack to get out of the hospital. Don't get me wrong. Ma was probably over the moon to have someone new to fuss over but if I was honest there was resentment under...scratch that. I was still furious with Esme's dad for putting her into contact with trash like Rojas to begin with. Then again, in the wee hours when I couldn't sleep and couldn't think straight anyway I thought——who knew if in some screwed up way I should be grateful? If Esme hadn't been running from Rojas that night, would we have met up again? It was a crazy thought but I still couldn't bring myself to put grateful and Gilberto Garcia in the same sentence. It was his daughter who showed courage and determination time and again throughout this whole disaster. She'd figured a way out of that jet, though she told me Rojas's driver had an attack of conscience and showed her where the baggage hatch was located. My fearless goddess. When I saw her climbing out of the rear baggage hatch I was scared shitless and proud of this badass woman at the same time. Bottom line—Esme was alive and in one piece and that was all that mattered.

"Seems there's a neighbor down the block from your parents looking to rent a basement apartment. No steps and a short walk to the beach. I'm going to paint it for him and he'll move in next week."

"You mean me, Leo and Finn will paint it." God knows the Fortunatos should be painters too for how often we offered our brawn to help out friends and family.

"We will. But not you. You're not even supposed to raise your left arm above your head."

I scoffed because she loved my macho act. "I can paint

better with one good arm than Finn and Leo together on their best days."

"Hmm. Maybe so. But they want to do it. Your family loves you, Shane."

"And what about you?" I'm such a needy sucker I have to hear the words. All the time.

"I guess they like me…" she teased, her green eyes glowing at her joke. When I emitted a sound that could only be called a growl, she relented. "Okay, okay, yes, mi amor, I love you. I always have, Shane. Never doubt it."

All I knew was I never needed another thing in this world if I had Esme. I'm riveted by her—always have been: her eyes, fearless and passionate, her hands, strong, graceful and damn, her words. I'm desperate to hear her say she wants me the way I want her— forever, desperate to keep her right here with me. With Esme and only with her I might be the man she thinks I am when she calls me her only one.

She squeezed onto the edge of the mattress and I grasped her hands, my thumbs tracing little circles in her soft palms. I swallowed a couple of times because emotions kept bombarding me like they have every day since Esme and I met up again. It's like I was only skimming the surface of my life before we reconnected. Love. All-consuming and as solid as our parents have for each other. Fear. I may never get over the abject terror that rips through me every time I think of what could've happened if things had gone down differently. God help me if I'd lost Esme after losing Chris. How would I go on? I didn't need the drama of the last few days as any kind of wake up call. I'd been convinced Esme meant every-thing to me for ten years. Every damn thing. But yeah, I was grateful. Grateful we were alive and together at last.

I used my elbows to shift to sitting, or I tried to, but Esme got all bossy. She put a light hand to my uninjured shoulder. "I'll raise the mattress," she said. She worked the buttons and levers of the bed like a pro and when she was done and I was sort of sitting up.

I pulled her toward me, nuzzling her neck. "My own personal nurse. I could get used to this." She swatted my hands away and backed up a few steps glancing over her shoulder at the door. I didn't care but I didn't blame her. We'd been interrupted a few times. If it wasn't my family it was a slew of cop friends or the investigators charged with figuring out how in hell it came to pass that Esme was stranded alone at the airport with Reinaldo Rojas. I have my own theory about how it could've happened and damn, if I'm right, it breaks my heart. My superiors tell me to let the investigators do their work. They'll get to the bottom of it— but I think maybe they will or maybe they won't because what happened at the airport proved Rojas's tentacles and money stretched further than anyone knew.

"Babe, come here, please." I thumped the mattress. "Sit next to me."

"Shane, you're still recovering."

"Nothing wrong with my lips, though."

She giggled even as she rolled her eyes at me, leaning in so her long hair swung out in an arc to cover both of our faces. I closed my eyes and breathed her in, angling my head slightly as I captured her lips. Needy, and so greedy, I used the tip of my tongue to stroke the seam of her lips. I slid my hand lightly under the sleek hair at her neck. My dream girl. When she moved in closer, resting her soft curves fully against my chest and granting me further access to her velvet mouth, I was lost in all things Esme.

The door burst open and before we could untangle ourselves, my family or part of them anyway, tumbled into the room. Jesus.

Ma, Pop, Finn and Ivy. My parents smiled big and I could read their collective mind. If I was well enough to be kissing

Esme, I was well enough. I agreed. Finn winked at me or tried to, his right eye had a lurid purple shiner. Ivy grinned and waved a naughty-naughty finger at us.

"We're staggering our visits today so as not to tire you," Ma said. "Leo, Delaney and Holly will make their way over tonight."

"Not that you look in the least tired," Ivy smirked.

"I'm tired of being here," I said. "But you guys don't have to keep visiting." *If they would just give me and Esme a little privacy.*

"You'll stay right here and without argument till the doctors tell you to go," Ma decreed, folding her arms across her chest. "Oh, if ye only knew how it pained a mother to see her child injured." Her gaze swept from me to Finn as she said it and I tried to forestall the incipient speech. If or when Finn quit boxing it had to be his decision. From my perspective he was just successful enough to think it was worth his while to continue.

Pop the peacemaker saved the day. "Esme made a delicious meal last night, something called chul..." he paused trying to pronounce the dish's name and Esme jumped in.

"Chuleta valluna." She lifted her hands like it was no big deal. "It's basically breaded pork."

"Nothing basic about it, honey," Pop said and Esme's cheeks flushed with pride. Pop was a more than decent cook in his own right so it was high praise.

"You're killing me over here talking about that while I'm stuck eating jello and cold soup," I said. "Where's my chuleta valluna?"

"S-s-sorry, bro, all gone." Finn chuckled.

Pop waved a placating arm. "Nah, I saved you some, Shane. A tiny portion." He raised a paper lunch bag. "Esme's not used to the Fortunato appetite. Next time we'll have to make twice as much." Esme's blush darkened to a deep rose

140

and I totally knew where her mind went with my father's remark about the Fortunato appetite. Our gazes collided and I raised a wicked brow.

When they all finally cleared out, Esme was the last to go. Her beautiful green gaze swung back to my face and I felt her examine it like she's done a million times since that horrible day, like she needed to be sure I was still here. "I have to pack up my father's things for discharge then tomorrow get him settled at your parents' house till his place is ready," she said.

"Okay but you'll come back later tonight? The rest of my siblings will be here after work so maybe you can come after that... like around eight right before visiting is over?"

"Of course, mi amor." She brushed her lush lips against mine and damn the twinge of pain, I put both arms around her and tugged her close, deepening the kiss with a grunt. Esme murmured in Spanish between kisses as she leaned in some more till her breasts were pushing against my chest.

"Ahgh. This... not being able to really hold you is killing me."

"Same. Doctor said one more day." She murmured the words against my lips before pulling back and brushing the hair back from my forehead with gentle fingers.

***

Esme

NOW I KNEW what the expression die a thousand deaths meant. I couldn't stop the dread that overtook me every time I left Shane, the desperate fear it might be the last time I saw him. When I closed my eyes at night, he was running across the tarmac, gun drawn, eyes fierce, intense and yes, looking

141

as terrified as I felt. Terrified for me. For us. I was beyond terror at that point. I'd spent every ounce of courage I possessed opening the back baggage compartment. After I landed on the ground I was out of ideas of how I would actually run away from Rojas—again. Besides, even I though wanted to run, I couldn't make my legs move. When Shane sprang out of nowhere and ran toward me with Rojas at the top of the steps screaming curses and threats, I instinctively followed his hand gesture and crouched behind the jet's tail.

When I slept, or tried to, every last detail of that horrendous day plowed through my mind on constant repeat. But I wasn't trapped in a theater forced to watch the kind of graphic movie I hated. The kind where the blood and gore was too realistic to be entertaining. I was living it. Over and over. The shrill explosive clatter of gunshots, the blinding, disorienting glare of the sun. My feeble attempt to disable the jet by slashing its tires until the ear-splitting barrage of bullets came so, so close, flashing silver and red while I watched petrified and powerless. And then...Shane getting hit. Shane falling to the ground but not before he discharged his weapon one last time causing Rojas to tumble down the jet's outer staircase.

When the EMS arrived I was the only uninjured person on the tarmac. They had to pry the switchblade out of my clenched fist. Shane had issued a feeble laugh and assured me he'd get me a new one.

So I'm not sleeping. How can I? There was Shane's surgery to remove the bullet and my father's treatment for his heart attack. We were all lucky to still be here. All the saints be praised as Clare Fortunato keeps saying. Shane was so sweet asking me if I would come back to see him again tonight. Silly man, doesn't he realize nothing would ever keep me away? He probably doesn't even know I slept in the chair by his bed the first night after he came out of surgery.

That Joe Fortunato retrieved me the next day from my post at Shane's side telling me his wife said. "Don't come back until you have Esme with you."

When I got back to St. Mary's before eight p.m. it was near both shift change and the end of visiting hours. At the nursing station I dropped off a tray of homemade lemon bars and oatmeal cookies, baked by yours truly and Shane's mom before I made my way down the hall to Shane's room. Everyone knew his story. Everyone knew he was shot stopping a bad guy and saving my life. Shane might not know I knew but there was an undercover officer minding his room, and my father's keeping everyone but vetted people out. There was a reason the original undercover plan went awry and Rojas wasn't arrested until the shootout with Shane. He wasn't lying when he boasted about having connections at every level of government. Someone with the clout to do it protected Rojas.

When I opened the door to Shane's room the lights were out but he wasn't in bed. My gaze swerved to the window where he was seated in a chair. For the first time since he got shot he was in street clothes, black jeans and a gray button down shirt that was not fully buttoned because of his bandages. He looked so good my mouth watered and I wished we were anywhere but here. When I shut the door behind me, he pushed to his feet.

"Shane. Don't stand up. You..." I hurried toward him but he was solid and steady on his feet.

"It's okay, Esme. I feel great. Stopped taking pain meds. Only taking the antibiotic now." It was then I noticed the faux pillar candle on the table beside him flickering a tiny amber light and the bud vase holding a single red rose.

"Where did those come from?" I asked the question with an edge to my voice because scruffy undercover Shane was unbelievably hot but cleaned up Shane resembled a naughty choirboy with his newly washed and brushed hair gleaming with deep auburn highlights. Did I have to make it clear to somebody on the staff both Shanes were mine? I'd been eager to get back to him but I was glad now I took the time to wash my hair and accepted Delaney's loan of jeans and a peasant blouse.

I hadn't been back to my apartment yet for clothing. Our place was an investigation scene with police tape stuck to the door and to be honest, I didn't think I'd ever go back without reliving every disgusting minute spent in Rojas's presence. Besides the Fortunatos were so welcoming. Here I was disrupting their lives but to hear Clare tell it, I was making life easier instead of the other way around. Shane's family possessed a warmth and such a gift for hospitality, they all made me feel I was doing *them* a favor by staying with them.

Shane's eyes gleamed like dark blue flames as he chuckled, his clean shaven jaw drawing attention to his sinful lips. "Babe, you're so good for my ego."

I folded my arms across my chest. "I see the way those nurses look at you. Which one helped you shower?" My face heated but I couldn't stop the words from tumbling out of my mouth. I was jealous as hell.

"Finn. Finn helped me shower and shave. He brought these clothes. And the rose and the candle. And you know, when Finn's in the room, no one bothers looking at me."

"Not true but okay, then." I forced my shoulders down, a little embarrassed by my outburst. Finnegan Fortunato is gorgeous by any standard but I've only ever had eyes for one Fortunato brother. Shane was my only one. "I would've helped you."

"Do I have to remind you about the one and only time… so far, we've been in the shower together?"

Delicious heat flooded my body at Shane's gruff words.

"Esme?"

144

"Shane?"

"Would you like to sit down and before you say anything the answer is—yes, Shane."

"But you're…"

Shane raised a brow.

"Yes, Shane."

He waved me into the chair he'd just vacated with his good arm. I sat, crossing one ankle-booted, also courtesy of Delaney's closet, leg over the other, hands folded in my lap. My gaze wandered over every inch of him from his polished black boots to ruddy color washing over his cheekbones. His eyes sparkled and he loomed tall and vigorous even if to my eyes there was a little less flesh on his finely corded muscles. Even with a bandage obscuring part of his clavicle and shoulder, it was hard to fathom he was recovering from surgery to remove a bullet from his shoulder.

When Shane cleared his throat I looked up and saw an unholy glitter in his eyes. "Eyes on my face, Esme. I know it's not easy with so much masculine perfection in front of you but give it the old college try, huh?"

I smirked, my face on fire but it pleased me beyond measure to see Shane looking so good and teasing me besides. I kept my gaze fixed on his face soaking in the sharp, angular planes, the little blue stud in his ear, the deep auburn waves brushing his collar. And then before my astonished eyes, he sank down onto one knee. My mouth dropped open when he pulled a ring from the chest pocket of his shirt.

"Esmeralda." He clasped my hands. "I've loved you since you were five years old. I didn't realize till you were fifteen it was the kind of love my parents have, your parents had…the forever kind. When you went away, at first I thought it was for the better. But I couldn't forget you…even though I tried. I finally told myself if we ever met again, I wouldn't waste time. I'd tell you how I felt. If things had gone differently this week, I might've lost you again." He swallowed, his Adam's apple working in his throat. "What I'm trying to say, Esme, is if you'll have me, I'll never leave you. I'll always love you, whatever the future holds. I'll do my best to give you the kind of life you deserve— love and protect you and any children we may have. Please say you'll marry me."

By the time Shane finished speaking tears were flowing freely down my face. I brushed them away with shaking hands but I couldn't stop them. Then we were both standing and my arms were tight around his waist.

"Shane." Wild tears sprang out again to flood his collar. "I can't sleep for thinking about how I almost lost you. I adore you. Seems like I've loved you forever. I always will."

"Then no more tears, Esme." He thumbed them away before sliding a delicate gold ring with two small emeralds on my ring finger.

"This is my mother's. It belonged to her mother who gave it to her before she emigrated to the states. She wants you to have it, she said from one immigrant woman to another. If it's not what you like, you can pick out something else but I'm…I don't want to wait. I want to marry you right away."

"I love it, Shane. If you mother is willing to part with it, that is."

He sank into the chair and pulled me onto his lap. I wiggled experimentally. "I'm not hurting you?"

"You're killing me, babe, if they don't discharge me soon…" He chuckled. "I can't wait to get you back to my place. Alone. Together. I want to get married as soon as we can get a license. It crossed my mind if I had…if things had gone south with Rojas, I wouldn't have provided for you. There wouldn't have been a death benefit for you."

"Shane, stop."

"No. This is a reality for a cop. My reality and now yours. And it's the reason I don't want to wait. Though actually how long I stay a cop is an open question. I'm on leave and not just because of this injury. They're investigating my role in in what went down at LaGuardia."

"*Your* role?" I sputtered. "You should be getting a commendation." Indignation had me jumping up before Shane's hand at my waist guided me back to his lap.

"I left my assignment. There are consequences for that kind of disobedience. All I can hope is the truth wins. At this point, the truth may be somewhere inside the NYPD, or with the Feds. Or who knows where. Let's hope we can find out. There's no getting round the fact Rojas must've had dirty people with influence on his payroll."

"He bragged about how he pays a lot of money to have free movement in this country."

"Yep." Shane smile was grim. "Anyway, I don't know what the future holds for my career. I could be out of a job soon. Sure you wanna a permanent hook up with a guy like me?" His lips quirked and I sifted a hand through his hair before I reached up to press my lips to his.

"So sure. Whatever happens, we figure it out together. You're all I want. You. You're my person, Shane. My only one. Everything else…" I lifted my hand in a sweeping motion and he grabbed it.

"Everything else will work out as long as we're together," Shane echoed, kissing my palm. "Forever."

THE END

Preorder Finn's story, *Say You're Mine*, Book 2 in The Fortunato Family series now at your favorite bookseller

ACKNOWLEDGEMENTS

This first book in the Fortunato Family series is also my first indie book. There are a ton of people to thank for their help in making this dream a reality.

Thank you to all of the indie authors I've met in person or virtually, who have generously answered questions, shared wisdom and insight and encouraged this moment. Donna Simonetta, Claire Marti, Peggy Jaeger, Sadira Stone and Katie O'Sullivan and many more, you know who you are —thank you for keeping me marginally sane.

To Charlie Coppa, First Officer, American Airlines. Thank you for you expertise.

To the amazing indie author Facebook groups and podcasters. I count on you for answers to every major or minor question about the craft of writing and indie publishing. You always come through with thoughtful, thorough responses. Many of you are famous, others are as new to this business as I am. I respect you all. We're in this together.

To romance readers: Thank you for picking up this book! I love romance—in whatever genre— as much as you do. I hope my stories thrill you with an escape from the everyday and an unforgettable happily ever after to savor.

To Mac and our family. Thank you for the constant encouragement and understanding when I'm lost in the clouds or bugging you with a technical question or needing an opinion. You take the time, every time to help me be better.

ABOUT THE AUTHOR

The only thing best-selling, award-winning author Charlotte O'Shay loves more than *reading* page-turning romance where happily ever after always wins is *writing* them. Charlotte lives with her real life hero, Mac in lower Manhattan where walks along the Hudson River serve up fresh story ideas every day.

Charlotte's writing has been called
"intoxicating, emotional and irresistible."
www.nnlightsbookheaven.com

Find out more about Charlotte's books at her website:
https://www.charlotteoshayauthor.com

Join Charlotte's list for first news of sales,
freebies and for general romance chit chat.
http://eepurl.com/b4LBvn